One Starry Knight

Christine E. Schulze

One Starry Knight

ONE STARRY KNIGHT
ISBN-13: 9798645856564

Christine E. Schulze
Copyright © 2015, 2018, 2020
Cover Art by Juney Nguyen © 2018

One Starry Knight

Praise for Schulze's
One Starry Knight on Goodreads

"A great story, I loved it."

~ *Pat, Goodreads*

"I liked the theme of redemption, forgiveness, and second chances throughout, and Kaos was a fascinating character."

~ *Sarah J., Goodreads*

"I haven't read a YA Fantasy quite like "One Starry Knight" and I applaud the author for ending the novel the way she did. It broke my heart!!"

~ *Ruby, Goodreads*

"I...like the author embracing diversity."

~ *Leena, Goodreads*

"What a lovely tale...I would read this one again and am more than willing to say that this is a book worth picking up, especially if you love a good fantasy and sweet romance...an unexpectedly sentimental book and one that I would read again. It's simplicity gave it a certain beauty and truthfulness not often found and it's ending had me more than a little willing to read more of Schulze's novels."

~ *Savannah Sutton, Goodreads*

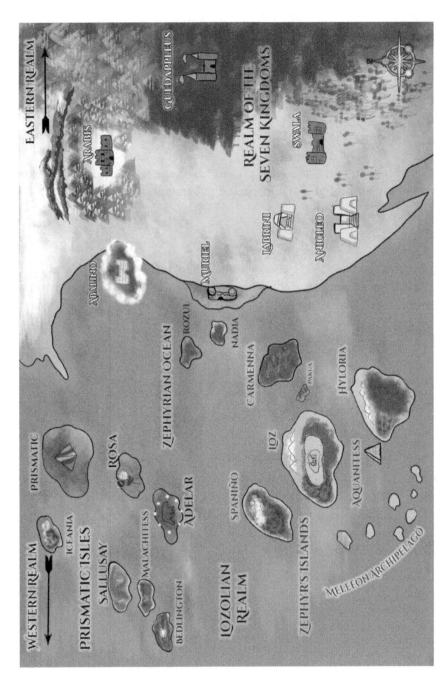

One Starry Knight

To my dear friend with the most beautiful spirit;
May the magic be with you wherever you go

One Starry Knight

1

Sir Kaos Jaspar made his strides long and fast as he trudged through the streets of Rozul.

The young knight with brown skin and hair dark as ebony scowled as he slipped through the crowds of Rozul people. He tried his best to avoid their suspicious glances—a feat which soon proved impossible. The sight of them disgusted him till he made himself stare instead at the cobblestone roads, still agleam with wetness from last night's rain. He was no fan of the Rozul, and they were clearly no fan of him, and they without reason. *He* was the stranger in *their* land. A novelty amongst their pale faces and judgmental spirits. They outnumbered him hundreds to one; he should fear them, not the other way around.

Of course, he had good sense to fear them to an extent and kept touching the pocket of his tunic to ascertain the bag of gold coins remained in check. He had secured this treasure after disposing of a much more valuable treasure that very morning—a dragon scale, to be exact. His sole purpose in coming to this wretched excuse for a kingdom. He had known he could catch the best price in Rozul, inasmuch as he had known to go to the pawn shop before dawn to make the trade, when as few eyes as possible would watch him.

As he neared the square, its hustle and bustle floated to him in a cacophony of cheers, shouts, jeers, a few cackles. He wondered what spectacle the square boasted today. Perhaps the circus was passing through as it had in Bedlington some weeks ago. Perhaps it was market day. He considered going the long way around to the southern woods and from there to the shore, but as a cart zoomed past, splashing mud on his freshly washed tunic, his desire to be rid of the place intensified. He picked up speed toward the square; cutting straight through would be the shortest, surest route to his destination.

No sooner had he reached the square than he was brought to a staggering halt by a thick wall of people encircling the wide-open space. Here, the people pressed so close they created a deafening roar of conversation and giddy laughter. Some shouted to one another from across the square, vainly expecting their targets to make sense of what they said.

Kaos used his strong, broad-shouldered girth to push his way through, taking no care of the sharp glares and foul names cast his way. The sooner he was past this vicious, narrow-minded rabble, the better. The sooner he could find the woods, and the ocean, and the south once again, the better. The south—*always* the south. South was now all that mattered.

As he pressed through the waves of crowds, he expected them to thin out, but they seemed to increase, both in number and in the compacted way they knit together. Bodies bumped against bodies, entwining like puzzle pieces trying to force themselves to fit with one another. With an irritated snarl, Kaos paused and looked up to see what exactly had the crowds so damn enthralled so early in the morning.

Several small, wooden platforms stood in the square's midst, constructed overnight by the shoddy look of them. Guards holding spears upright surrounded the platforms. Young men and women, as well as several children, stood on the platforms. They were all clad in thin tunics, most so tattered as to hardly be considered rags. Some had been scrubbed clean head to toe, so that their skin shone red. Bruises and smudges of dirt covered others. All wore bonds around their wrists, if not their ankles too—ropes, twine, some even wore chains. Men more finely clothed walked around the platforms, introducing those dressed in rags with all the dignity of one describing livestock—their weight, birth date, type of labor, strengths, weaknesses—and commencing bids.

The slave market. This realization, coupled with the immensity of the crowds that had gathered and the interest with which they watched, fueled Kaos' anger anew. Barging roughly past the couple nearest him, he continued his fight through the throngs toward the other side of the square and the freedom beyond—

In the blink of an eye, Kaos found his attention fixated to a small white form between the crowds and stopped short. He squeezed forward a few steps, staring at the young woman on display. Her hair fell in long, bright, gold-red waves. Her eyes were an impossible shade of green and shimmered almost like they were made of crystal. Their color was impossible because they matched those exactly of *her*...*his* her. The *her* who should have never had green eyes, so rare was such a trait amongst his people...

But *her* time was long past. It was this slave girl's eyes that called to him now—this girl with the wild red hair, milk white skin, and too-thin, willowy frame. Her skin was clean as snow, but her master had not seen fit to give her a proper gown; she wore a simple white peasant's frock, dingy, tattered, and torn.

Her bedraggled frock contrasted strangely not only with her ethereal beauty, but especially with the gem hanging around her neck on a golden chain; it was a sizeable gem, pink in color, and its facets glistened with gold, orange, and purple hues in the sunlight—almost as though she had kidnapped a sunset or sunrise and hidden it inside.

The longer Kaos studied her, the more deeply he decided: She would be his redemption—his atonement. She would replace the one he had lost, and he would not lose her.

Kaos waited patiently. When every other slave on the platform had been sold, the auctioneer turned his attention to the green-eyed girl and declared,

"And here we have saved the best for last! A young lady, about eighteen or nineteen years of age. A picture of eternal youth..."

Kaos let the cold descriptions fade to the back of his mind till he saw only her beauty, and beyond that, her fear. She stood very still, straight, demure. She was a lady, or perhaps *had* been once, before fate had dealt her such an unkind hand. Beyond her calm reserve, fear shone clearly in her eyes. She feared being dealt the same kind of fate again, or perhaps an even crueler one.

"*...and* this lovely lady is the property of none other than our revered Master Brant!"

Excitement rippled tangibly through the crowds who turned their gaze briefly in another's direction. Kaos found the man standing to the side of the platform and felt his heart bristle at the sight of him. Ridiculously clad

in bright silks, gold, and gems, Master Brant was possibly the most richly dressed individual present. He watched his property hungrily, almost with spite, as if letting her go pained him greatly. Men of such power and status often had only one purpose for enslaving such a beautiful young woman. Kaos suddenly thought it would give him overwhelming joy to be the cause of this man's pain.

"...let the bidding commence at ten gold coins! Ten gold coins for the lovely lady and her rare magic gem!"

As if the auctioneer's words were some magic command spell—or perhaps the spell lay hidden in the girl's green eyes—Kaos' hand shot into the air, along with the hands of many others. He glanced about the crowds, trying to size up the immensity of his competition, but his attention was drawn once more to Master Brant. A young man, a servant perhaps, now stood beside him. A new fierceness illuminated Master Brant's eyes as he surveyed the hands lifted high all around, eager to snatch his treasure away from him.

"That gem ain't magic!" a woman shouted from the crowds. "If *I* had a magic gem, I'd 'ave used it to slay all ya bastards by now and be rid o' ya!"

"Do not dare to speak such disrespect toward his honor, Master Brant!" another woman shouted. "'Tis treason to even suggest—"

"Never mind if it's magic or not!" a man cried. "A gem that size will catch more than a generous share of gold. I bid fifteen, good sir!"

"I have fifteen gold coins!" the auctioneer shouted. "Will anyone raise the bidding to twenty?"

"Twenty," Kaos shouted. Murmurs of disapproval rippled through the crowds. Kaos ignored them. He kept his hand raised high, and his gaze suddenly locked with the maiden's. She stared back as if equally spellbound.

"The young Carmennan man bids twenty—do I hear twenty-five?"

"Twenty-five!" shouted the man who had bid fifteen.

"Twenty-six," Kaos said. More murmurings and irritated glares turned in his direction.

"Twenty-sev—"

"Thirty."

The irritation waving through the crowds steadily turned to hushed whispers of incredulity. Was the young Carmennan mad? Could they

11

suppose that he, in his plain black tunic, had the funds necessary? Was he calling bluff?

"Thirty-one," called a woman from the crowd.

"Thirty-two," an older man said.

"Forty," Kaos declared.

The numbers flew, mounting toward one hundred. More and more hands and bids joined. And then, as the numbers climbed past one hundred, more and more hands and bids receded until there was only Kaos and two others.

"Two hundred gold coins," one man declared with a sneering finality in his voice. He was very certain of himself. Kaos glanced about; the Rozul were *all* so certain, so confident in themselves. The idea that he, an outsider, could steal their prize was absurd to them, to the point of being impossible. He would keep the bids going, he would string the people along, keep them sweating, keep them guessing till the last second...

But then his gaze drew back to *her*. To the infinite pleading in her steady green gaze. He didn't know whether she begged him to win her or lose her. But he knew who he was, that he sought only to take care of her and keep her safe. The sooner she was with him, the sooner she could know this too, and the sooner she could breathe a sigh of relief, at least in terms of her safety—and at least until the secrets of the north caught up with him...

No. No, he would have her secured far in the south by then, safe within the Sealing.

"Two hundred ten," he shouted.

"Two hundred fifty," his competitor returned; the other man lowered his hand with a scowl.

Kaos took a deep breath. He felt the weight of the bag at his side, just beneath his cloak. He felt the sword in its hilt at his other side, just in case. It was time to deal the final blow.

"Three hundred gold coins."

"Impossible," his rival sneered, while gasps, mutterings, even a few chuckles rose from the crowds. "Not a man alive aside from noblemen like myself—or his lordship, Master Brant—would cart such a hefty sum around. This ragtag ruffian from the 'isle of music and dreams' is clearly not only a dreamer, but delusional as well, and a liar—"

Kaos marched forward—the crowds parted like a wave—and threw the bag of gold, which landed right on the edge of the platform. As a few coins spilled from the bag and rang on the ground below, a more enthusiastic wave of gasps echoed around the square. Some of the front-most townsfolk dove to retrieve the coins, but guards quickly leapt between them and their prize, warding them off with crossed spears.

The auctioneer stepped forward and, with a groan, hefted the bag of gold coins. One of the guards handed him the stray coins, and he held them in his hand, turning them over. A gleam of desire flashed in his eyes, but then he shoved the coins inside the bag, descended the platform, walked over to Master Brant, and said, "Three hundred gold coins, my lord. Shall we strike the trade here with..?" He turned back to Kaos.

"Sir Kaos Jaspar," he said.

"...with Sir Kaos Jaspar?"

Master Brant's gaze roamed the girl's body a final time. Kaos let his fingertips inch toward his sword, ready at any moment to draw his blade. He wasn't about to be swindled out of three hundred gold coins—certainly the most money he had ever owned in his life—especially not after the turmoil that had birthed their acquirement. Nor would he let the pig whose lusting glance continued to consume the girl take her back. Kaos flexed his muscles as subtly as he could, cracked his knuckles, his neck. He could do with a good fight, at any rate. The girl had closed her eyes and stood taking deep breaths. Her lips moved, as if she muttered a prayer. Her desperation angered Kaos further; if this fool of a man didn't make up his mind soon...

"If you need to count them, milord," Kaos said stiffly. "But I assure you, the full sum is there—"

"Done," Master Brant released in a heavy sigh. Defeat and frustration twisted his face into a nasty frown. He shot Kaos an ugly glare before nodding toward the auctioneer and declaring, "Release her to her new master."

The auctioneer nodded toward a man clad in a simple tunic, no doubt another servant. The servant grabbed the ropes imprisoning the damsel's wrists and pulled her toward the steps. She staggered, her ankles yet bound together as well. Kaos rushed over to meet her, pushing past the crowds who gathered close to get a better view.

The servant hurried down the steps, yanking the rope as he went. The girl fell, but Kaos darted forward to catch her by the shoulders and steady her. Glaring past her at the servant, he said, "She is mine now. I'll thank you to take care with her." He jerked the rope from the servant's hands.

"Milord," the servant muttered, before scurrying back up the platform to the auctioneer's side.

Kaos turned back to his new ward. His hands still rested on her delicate shoulders, and it took every ounce of his will to resist drawing her forward into a tight embrace. Her long waves of sun-kissed hair, her willowy frame—everything except her snow-white skin mirrored the one who had come before. His other *her*. Especially those otherworldly green eyes staring up at him, expectant yet uncertain. The fear in those eyes reminded him who she really was, made him release his touch on her shoulders and take a step back.

Then, drawing a knife from his belt, Kaos cut the ropes binding the maiden's wrists. Kneeling down, he freed her ankles as well. Anger flitted through him again at the sight of red markings on her tender flesh, raw and with the skin torn away in places. How long had they kept her this way?

It didn't matter, he told himself, as he stood to his feet and sheathed the knife. All that mattered now was protecting her and going south.

Always south.

Placing an arm around her, he began guiding her through the crowds, away from the square. The sounds of other auctions commenced, fading behind them the further they drew from the accursed place. Kaos picked up pace, wondering if she would be able to keep up, but she did well enough, almost running to match his long strides. An eagerness gleamed in her eyes, a sudden fire leapt to life; she was just as keen as him to put the square behind her.

No sooner had they emerged into the street beyond than Master Brant ran up from behind them and intercepted their path. His servant trailed close on his heels and stumbled to a stop beside him, panting hard as he tried to catch his breath.

Master Brant's gaze locked on the girl. His eyes were lit with a sudden wild desperation, as though he had made some grave mistake in getting rid of her and sought now to correct it.

Kaos held the maiden closer to him and let his free hand trail to his sword; he quickly tired of this man's pursuit and now took a moment to size him up. No apparent sword or other weapon to speak of, yet the bright colors and rich fabrics of his garb suggested that he had power enough to rain every single guard in Rozul down on them. The girl trembled head to toe beside Kaos, clutching her pendant. She kept a steady gaze locked on her old captor, looking alarmed but brave, ready to face him.

"May I help you, Master Brant?" Kaos asked, his voice tight, though he tried to sound as pleasant as he could; the matter of the girl's safety was reason alone to stave any kind of fight, but time was also of the essence. For the sake of her safety, they *must* be on the move.

Master Brant continued to stare at the girl. A sort of rage glinted in his eyes. His lips pursed tightly together, as if ready to burst with the words filling him, and yet he seemed unable to speak them. His face turned bright red, and Kaos thought the man might literally explode—which wouldn't be an altogether terrible fate for such a man, in Kaos' opinion.

More loudly, Kaos said, "Milord. Master Brant, what can we do for you?"

Master Brant seemed entranced a moment longer. Then, as if Kaos' words finally broke through and severed whatever spell held him silent, he released his breath in one giant exhale. He drew several deep, exasperated breaths. His entire body became rigid, fists clenched. At last he said, with clear disdain in his voice, "I warn you, while she may be lovely to look at, that is as far as her loveliness extends. If you did not buy her for a pretty-looking housemaid, I am afraid you'll be sorely disappointed."

"But *you* won't," Kaos said. He let his fingertips hover over the hilt of his sword, tempted to spear the man through anyway if he kept staring at the girl with all the contempt of a man staring at a pile of filthy rags. "You have your three hundred gold coins. We'll be on our way."

Master Brant continued to stare at the girl. His servant fidgeted, glancing uneasily between him and the knight whose irritation fast mounted into an anger that his master seemed unable to recognize as he focused on his old prize.

Then, at last, Master Brant tore away and walked past, roughly brushing shoulders with the girl and muttering, "Yes. I suppose you shall..."

Kaos flung a sharp glance over his shoulder, watching as Master Brant disappeared back into the crowds along with his servant, no doubt to claim another pretty face in place of the one he had just lost. His hand flexed over his sword; if only he had the power to free them all...

But he must go south. South must be his sole focus. Especially now, with the maiden at his side.

"Come," he said, drawing her along. "Let us get as far from this accursed place as quickly as possible."

On they wound through the streets, catching the alarmed, intrigued, or, more times than not, judgmental glances of the Rozul people. Kaos pushed past them, increasing his speed and letting that be the release of the pent-up energy pulsing inside him. He touched his sword, then let go. The temptation was too strong. The sooner he freed himself from the sight of these vile excuses for human beings, the better.

Of a sudden, he noticed that he seemed more to drag her with him, whereas before she had easily matched his pace. He paused long enough to glance at her, at the quiet pain in her eyes, at the trail of blood smudged on the pavement behind them. Perhaps *this* was why the people glared at him like some kind of monster. He hadn't realized she wore no shoes.

Sweeping her up into his arms, he carried her the rest of the way through town, until at last they emerged into the woods beyond. She cuddled close against him, her arms wrapped around his neck. He inhaled deeply, overcome for a moment by the sweet scents of whatever oils her body had been adorned with for the occasion. Long months had passed since he had held the comfort of a woman in his arms.

Finding the small stream he sought, he set her on the ground, with her feet dangling in the clear water. Then, kneeling beside her, he began washing her feet. How delicate they were, hardly bigger than his hands.

Gently, he ran his hands over them. She winced and drew a sharp breath, and he withdrew his touch, letting the water do the work for him instead. He waited until most of the blood had washed away. Then, carefully, he swung her feet from the water, scooped mud from the river's bed, and began packing it onto the soles of her feet. Blisters covered them in places, and the tender layers of skin had been stripped altogether in others. Their run through town clearly wasn't the only source of her pain, but all the same, Kaos couldn't stave his overwhelming guilt. Once more, he had let his own temper and desires make him neglect the care of another. With the mud packed on, Kaos wrapped each of her feet in a thick layer of soft leaves which he then secured with reeds.

"I am sorry," he said. "But this should help heal and protect them till we reach the next town. I will get you some proper shoes, but not here—I believe we may have made more enemies here in a day than I have in my entire lifetime."

"The Rozul see everyone outside their insular race as enemies," the maiden said, all the while staring up at him with a sort of bewilderment.

For a moment, Kaos sat thrown off guard and stared back with a similar incredulity. Her voice was quiet, as he had expected for such a small being, but etched with an unusual strength and ringing with an almost musical quality, like chimes or bells. Her voice seemed almost to sparkle, just like the gem about her neck.

He took both her slender hands in his rough, broad ones and drew her slowly to her feet. Keeping his gaze locked on hers, spellbound by their bright green stare, he kissed her hands—one, then the other—and said, "Milady—and what shall I call you?"

"Evren," she released the name in a single breath, like a sigh she had been holding inside her for some time. She continued to stare at him, not so much bewildered now as captivated. Her wonderment made him intrigued by her in turn, yet uneasy at the same time.

"And what shall I call *you*, good sir?" she asked quietly.

"I am indeed a knight. But I do not wish to be called 'sir.' You may call me 'Kaos.'"

"Kaos," she said. "A curious name for a knight."

"As Evren is a curious name for a such a small creature as yourself—does it not mean 'heavens' or 'universe' in some ancient language?"

Evren nodded. "But even the smallest person may hide the biggest secrets. My grandmother used to tell tales of a lad who swallowed an entire city just to keep his family safe."

"Then perhaps your grandmother also knew tales of knights and could guess that 'Kaos' is not what men would call my 'rightful name.'"

"She likely could. But if not Kaos, then what and why..?"

"Kaos is not the name I was born with, but it is the only name I now know. A knight may change his name, if he himself has changed enough so that he no longer resembles the man to which his old name once belonged..."

Kaos' gaze strayed then to the pendant hanging just above her heart. He gently took it in his hand and turned it over. Sunlight reflected brilliantly on its sunset-colored hues. He admired it a few moments longer before her hand darted out and snatched it from him. She stared up at him, a wildfire blazing in her eyes as she clutched the pendant tight.

"Forgive me for alarming you," Kaos said. "I would not take your treasure; of that I can assure you. I was only curious... Master Brant seemed disappointed to be rid of you, and yet he seemed incapable of reclaiming you. Strange, for a man with such power..."

"The gem *might* be magic after all, yes," Evren said, still holding it firmly. "But if it is, then only I know how to use it."

"Did you? To get away from him?"

"I made a wish. The wishes have a will of their own, otherwise I would have fled long ago. They are limited in number, and one cannot trust them to do exactly as one has in mind. But I did make one, and it helped, I think."

Kaos studied her a few moments more. He reached up slowly, played with a lock of her hair. It ran through his fingers softer than any velvet he had ever touched, warm and shining as if made of pure sun. He cupped one of her cheeks, touched his thumb to her chin. He tilted her face up just a bit toward his, considering. She watched him expectantly, but if she used any wish to separate them, he did not feel its power.

Then, lowering his hand, he drew away and said, "Come. We head south."

2

Evren followed her new master in silence as they continued to delve more deeply into the woods. The sun had since dipped nearly below the horizon, and traces of stars began to creep along the highest fringes of the darkening sky. Most eyes would not yet detect them, but Evren's always did.

A dull throbbing continued to pulse in her feet, but the mud cooled them, lessening the pain. She shivered as the night's cool air descended but made no complaints. Her new master had thus far been much more generous to her than her previous had ever been. Kaos was a most fascinating creature, and she trailed behind him just a bit, the better to study him without showing disrespect or making him feel uncomfortable at her intensely focused gaze; such expressions of curiosity had brought her much misery at the hands of Master Brant. She did not think this new master would be so cruel, but especially because of his kindness, she did not wish to alarm him. Thus, she studied him in silence, and at a bit of a distance.

A fierce determination was hard-set in his midnight eyes; Kaos was a man of purpose. His skin was dark brown like the earth and shone in the starlight filtering between the trees with what seemed an ethereal beauty to her; between the Rozul and her own people with their milky white skin, she had never before seen such a lovely creature. His broad frame, etched with obvious muscle and strength, made her feel safe; he was an ample bodyguard. But her gaze kept straying to his hands with a longing for the surprising gentleness of their touch to return to her.

"Are you hungry?" Kaos asked suddenly, coming to a halt.

Evren stopped beside him and nodded. "A little…"

Kaos stooped low to the ground. Drawing out a short knife, he clipped a branch from one of the bushes brushing the ground. Then, he held up a cluster of small red fruits.

"Strawberries!" she exclaimed. "My favorite."

"Are they?" He arched a skeptical brow.

"Yes, along with blackberries—and you needn't look at me that way. You'll find I am a poor liar."

Kaos nodded and granted a subtle grin. "In that much, we are the same. Sit, eat. I'll pick us some more for now, and for our journey ahead."

Evren did as she was told, drawing aside several fallen branches to find a soft spot on the earth. Kaos sat beside her, clipping berries from the bushes and setting them down between the two of them.

"Is there anything I can do to help?" Evren asked.

Kaos glanced up at her, looking surprised, even a bit annoyed. "No. Thank you. But you are not my servant. If anything, in rescuing you, I am yours."

As he continued cutting berries from the bush, Evren stared back with greater surprise. "You mean…do you not intend..?" She reached out, placed her hand on his.

He tensed, and then jerked away. With a sharp glare, he said, "No. That is *not* my intent. I would never take a maiden against her will. My honor as a knight, and as a man, defies the very idea—though some would do so to make themselves feel like more of a man, and in doing so make themselves less."

Kaos returned his gaze to his work, seeming almost to rip the berries from the earth, and Evren fell silent. As she watched him, she noted the long scars crisscrossed up and down his arms and wondered at their source; it looked like long claws or knives might have created them. The sight caused her pain, so that she wanted to reach out and wrap them in a healing balm as he had her feet, even though, by their color and fadedness, they were old scars, not in need of any real tending.

Her glance strayed then to his sword, which he had laid right beside him. It nestled inside a black leather sheath so that only the hilt was visible. The black and white bands patterned within the silver hilt fascinated Evren. The silver looked smooth but didn't shine quite as brightly as silver normally would.

"Your sword," she said. "The hilt—it's unlike any silver I've ever seen."

"Because it isn't," Kaos said. "It's jasper stone."

"Jasper...like your family name."

He nodded and offered a small smile. "Exactly."

Evren smiled back. "I used to collect rocks. We lived by an old seer. She and my grandmother were great friends. I would bring my rocks to her, and she would tell me their names and meanings. *My* jasper stone had bands of brown and gold. Anyway, she said jasper was a symbol of strength and healing."

The hint of a smile lingered in Kaos' eyes, though he did not let it show fully on his face this time. He only said, "Fascinating as that is, all the jasper in the world won't help us if we don't also eat to keep up our strength. Finish your meal so we can be on our way. There will be plenty of time for talk later."

They finished eating in silence and then continued through the woods. Darkness soon enclosed the forest, but the sky was clear of any clouds and the stars shone with an unparallel brilliance. Evren could make out hundreds of thousands spanning in all directions beyond the trees. Their light filtered brightly through the branches, easily lighting their path—

She stumbled against Kaos, who had once more come to a halt.

"Sorry," she said.

"It's all right," he muttered, fishing around beneath his cloak. "I was hoping I still had a bit of oil left; we could create a torch. It's blacker than the pits of hell with all these trees, and my eyes aren't what they used to be."

"Let me lead the way."

He glanced at her first with cynicism, then curiosity. Nodding at her pendant, he said, "More magic?"

Evren studied him closely for a moment, considering. "Yes, more magic," she said at last, then took the lead. "We just keep going south?"

"Yes. Take us south."

Evren led the way for the next while of their journey. She took them by the easiest paths she could find, warning him of thorn bushes or hidden holes or other snags and dangers. After another hour or so, judging by how the stars had shifted overhead, they emerged onto a shore sprinkled with pebbles and fireflies and with a great, wide river spanning before them.

"Well done," Kaos said, with clear amusement. "This is exactly where we should be. We will cross, then camp and make for the ocean tomorrow. We cannot take the river from here to the ocean; the rapids and falls leading there are too treacherous."

He started walking down the shore, and Evren turned to ask him how they would cross, but her attention was immediately snared by the sight of the woods from which they had just come. Between the dark shapes of the trees, hundreds of bright, sparkling lights bedazzled her eyes, like stars she could reach out and take in her hands, or like the fireworks she had glimpsed outside her cell window once. She crept closer, watching their magic glisten before her and wondering how she had not seen the lights before, when she and Kaos were inside the trees.

"The fireflies." Kaos was suddenly beside her. "They come out at a certain time every night. They look like stars, don't they? They're perhaps the one beautiful thing about this island. But come. I found the boat."

Kaos walked away from her again. Evren stared at the woods a moment longer, stunned that the lights of such tiny creatures could create such a special phenomenon.

She turned and followed Kaos to the shallows where a row boat now rested. Thick markings in the earth showed where he had dragged it from some hiding place in the trees. He offered his hand and she took it, climbed inside. Then, he pushed off from the shore and began rowing.

"Kaos," Evren said. It felt peculiar, saying his name, when she had been forced to call all "master" over the past several months. But it was quite nice to say too; it made her feel as though they could almost be friends. The sound of it rolling off her tongue made a strange, bright bit of happiness flit through her, so that she said again, "Kaos. May I ask you a question?"

He glanced down at her with sudden hesitation. Then he stared out before him again, across the river and into the woods beyond. "I cannot promise to hold the answers you seek, but I can promise honesty inasmuch as I can grant an answer."

"Why…why did you rescue me?" Evren asked. "Why spend so much on someone you obviously don't need around? I am not your mistress. I'm no good with a sword or a bow, even had you given me one."

"I saved you because Rozul's customs disgust me," Kaos said, spitting over the side of the boat and glaring at the land they had just set sail from, so hard that his eyes might have burned a hole straight through the trees. "The mere idea of slavery disgusts me. Our King Mikanah and Queen Lorelei rid Carmenna of all slavery as soon as they reclaimed the throne from Moragon. I'm sure you've heard of Moragon, the false king—he enslaved most of my people with music and mental tricks. He abused his power—the power he stole in the first place. No one in Carmenna is allowed now to sell any human being for any purpose or use any means of mental magic to control them."

"You've done this before then?" Evren asked. "Rescued slave girls from the market?"

"No. I don't make a point of visiting Rozul on a regular basis. It was a necessary stop in my path; I had business to attend here before journeying on. Before that, I had gone as far south as possible without making any stops. Seeing you in the market... It was fate, I suppose. Perhaps Amiel himself provided me a means of atoning for my sins by allowing me to save *you*, instead of..."

"Instead of..?" she dared to press.

For a while, he said nothing, and Evren didn't think he would. She stared into the black depths of his eyes, at the stars reflected within. Beyond his somberness, she caught the briefest glimmer of the same passion that had blazed in his eyes from when he had first espied her right up till the moment he had obtained her. The hard-set features of his face softened just a little, giving a slight whimsical touch to his appearance, and he said, "I want to show you something. Lay down in the boat."

Evren hesitated. It seemed a strange request for him to make. She didn't distrust him. She didn't fear that he might have ill intentions in making such a demand; thus, she found herself so intrigued, unable to imagine for what reasons he might make his request. After pondering a few moments more, she complied and lay down in the boat. Kaos moved to the side of the boat and stood there. Evren sprawled on her back, shifting so that the boat's wooden planks cradled her as comfortably as they could. She was about to tell him that she was ready and ask what he wanted her to see, but then she watched him place the oar in the water, continue rowing, and glance at her before turning his gaze to the heavens. She followed his gaze and instantly fell into an enchanted silence.

In the great Rozul city, where she had only ever known the confines of a small, dank room beneath one of the houses, she had hardly seen the stars, save to glimpse them from a tiny window now and then. She had been able to view them only as a handful at a time.

Now, however, they stretched above and around her like an endless ocean. Hundreds upon thousands upon millions, weaving countless stories, patterns, pictures, galaxies, colors, and shapes to create one glorious and ever-expanding universe. Up there, anything was possible.

Slowly, the boat spun, around and around. The stars swirled past, over and over again. The sight of them calmed Evren and exhilarated her at once. She reached for them, letting her hands dance in and out of their patterns as Kaos continued to command the boat to perform its circular waltz. She could almost imagine that she could touch the stars, part them like a veil, and step inside them into another world.

"My grandmother used to tell legends about the stars," she said quietly.

"Did she?" Kaos prompted gently.

Evren nodded, keeping her gaze locked on the stars spinning above her. "She told legends of a world called 'Novalight.' In Novalight, she said, men and women just like you and me actually became Stars, and the Stars would guard Novalight from above, protecting it and all who lived within. The Stars were said to be extraordinarily strong, both in a physical

27

and spiritual sense. Some had special gifts; in watching the whole world from the sky, they gained a unique perspective on everything and could gaze out into the future in a way others couldn't. But as strong as they were, sometimes even they would get sick, and fall to Novalight. Fallen Stars, they were called. And their only way back to the heavens was to sacrifice themselves for another. To use their Starfire—their life source— to save another's life... They would die then as humans, but to be resurrected as a Star once more, never to fall again."

"Your grandmother's story is beautiful—as is your necklace."

Only as he spoke the words did she realize she had been fiddling with the pendant hanging about her neck. "It was also my grandmother's. She said the stone is called a 'sunstone,' made from a powerful Star, a queen who ruled as another planet's sun for some time..." She smiled up at Kaos. "It's nice, sharing these stories with someone."

Kaos still studied the heavens, and his face had pulled once more into its solemn frown. "And your grandmother?"

"I don't know. I don't know about any of my family. All I have known the past several months is Rozul and the slave market. I've had no chance of escape, of finding what might have become of them. Not that I would know how to reach them, or even how far I am from them. No one was ever to pay so high a price as Master Brant demanded till *you* came along."

"The money was not acquired by happy means," Kaos said. "I was not unhappy to part with it, and especially for the purpose of saving your life."

He brought the boat to a halt then sent it moving in a straight line once more. Evren remained where she was, content to watch as the stars glided past above them.

She was almost lulled to sleep by their serene passing when the boat stopped with a gentle jolt. She sat up and combed a hand through her thick waves of hair. Kaos helped her from the boat then set about dragging it into the woods to hide. Evren followed him, eager to help should he need any, though she doubted her small strength could be of much use to him.

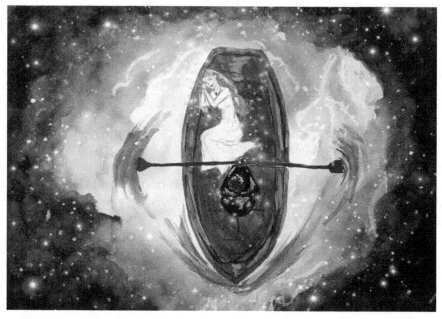

Once Kaos had secured the boat beneath a cleverly constructed pile of branches and vines, he nodded with satisfaction at his work and brushed his hands off on his tunic. Then he turned to her and said, "Ready? We'll head in a little ways more then find a safe place to camp for the night."

Without giving her time to answer, he turned and started on his way again, but Evren reached out, touched his arm, and said, "Wait. Please."

He tensed then turned to look at her.

"Yes, milady?"

Evren's heart skipped inside her—a familiar feeling, yet so rusty as to seem foreign to her—as he bestowed this special title upon her a second time and studied her sharply with his dark, far-reaching eyes.

"I just wanted to thank you," she said softly. "Thank you for saving me and keeping me safe. And for showing me the stars."

She crept close and slowly reached up to caress his face. The slightest tenderness, one deeply buried, touched his hard-set gaze, melting away some of its solemnity. He reached his hands to hers and pressed them to his cheeks—

Only to grab her wrists the next moment, yanking her back from him so abruptly that she stared up at him as stunned as if he had slapped her. The solemnity returned to his gaze ten-fold, along with a fierceness that made her shudder. Tension pulsed through his rigid, stalwart frame, though his voice was quiet and even as he spoke:

"I did rescue you. And I will care for you. But there are rules. Very few in number—but unbreakable in nature. I may kiss you, if you like. I would be intimate with you, to comfort us both. But I will never hold you. Because I will never fall in love with you. We will not fall in love with each other."

"Then I will not be intimate with you," Evren said, swallowing hard and blinking back unexpected tears as the words spilled from her with an equally unexpected boldness. "I could only choose to be intimate with someone who loves me, and I him."

Kaos gave a single nod. "Good. Then we are agreed and understand one another."

He checked the ropes on the boat a final time. Then, he trudged into the woods, making long strides so that she had to hurry to keep up.

"Kaos," she said, "where are we going really?"

"South," he said. "Always south."

"What's south?"

"Away. South is away."

"Away..?"

"Away from everything."

His voice rang with a certain finality, and Evren determined to follow him in silence from that point on. She allowed herself to fall back a couple of feet, to wipe away the tears that, with their new understanding, she decided he was not allowed to see.

After a little while, they emerged from the woods into a wide open plain. The black sky spanned before them, bedazzled still with millions of stars. For a moment, on the boat, Evren had seen those stars in Kaos' eyes. She had let herself believe that she could catch them. But now his words promised that, just like the stars above them, no matter how long and far she kept reaching, her hands would never close around them. His light and warmth would never be hers to hold. Perhaps another had extinguished it long ago; perhaps it no longer existed.

Whatever the case, feeling too strongly was something she could not afford at present. This was her home now, at his side. She must do her best to serve this young knight who had rescued her, and she could not do so by letting her passion get the best of her.

She decided to close that tender place in her heart that had begun to open. She ignored its ache, stitching up the fresh wounds that had begun to form at his rejection before they could have the chance to bleed more readily.

Only then, when she considered the walls surrounding her heart built as solidly as his, did she hurry her pace to walk alongside him.

3

Thus, their journey continued.

Within a couple days' time, they had reached the southernmost borders of Rozul where Kaos revealed another boat he had hidden. As they climbed in, Evren wondered aloud whether such a small craft would hold them as they ventured across the mighty ocean. Kaos only assured they had not far to go before reaching land again.

Indeed, after surviving a week or so on fish, berries, and other foods Kaos had scrounged up before setting sail, the shores of a massive island loomed into view. "Loz," Kaos called it. Evren stared out with excitement at the rising mountains covered with trees and the village set in the hills and shore below. Rozul had been the only place she had known in these parts, but she had heard great things of Loz, of its beauty, justice, and the diversity of people who lived there. She hoped they might stay at the quaint little seashore village for a while and do some exploring.

But, even upon docking at Loz, they were ever on the move.

Evren had hoped a new location might calm Kaos, make him less restless. Now and again, she would ask him what exactly their destination was as they trudged through woods, fields, or various towns without so much as stopping to spend the night or talk to a single soul. Each time, she was met with the same response: "South." Always south. Evren wondered what was in the south. Or what was in the north that he had declared they must flee. But she never asked. It was silently understood between them that she didn't ask, and if she did, that asking would bear no answers.

In fact, they spoke truly little to each other over the course of the next few days. They had spoken little on the voyage to Loz, and Evren had understood. The sailing had been smooth, but there hadn't been much food and water to divide between the two of them, leaving them both in less than pleasant moods and Kaos more brooding than he had been even at the start.

This mood seemed to carry over as they delved deeper into the southern woods of Loz. Kaos hadn't called her "milady" since that second time. He hardly even looked at her. Evren wondered what she might have done to upset him but couldn't find courage to ask. She instead tried to make herself as useful as she could, absorbing his every silent lesson on gathering safe berries, shrooms, and herbs to eat; trapping rabbits and other small beasts; and fishing and other practicalities necessary for their survival.

On their second week in Loz, they entered a village rather larger than any they had yet encountered. It was another seaside town. The buildings were constructed of wood and stone and surrounded by many trees; some of the buildings nested up in the very trees themselves.

As soon as they entered town, Kaos seemed to pick up pace. His posture straightened, and his somber gaze brightened just a bit, as if they had crossed some invisible barrier Evren could not comprehend.

"Where are we?" she asked, hurrying to match his pace. Her feet had begun to hurt again, though Kaos kept the mud and makeshift shoes as fresh as he could.

"The Forest-footer town of Willardton. I have many old friends who live here. I will be able to trade some of the animal skins we've collected for food and a few coins—enough for us to find lodging for the week."

"Don't we need to keep moving?" Evren ventured. "South? What about the south?"

"Even the south can wait for Willardton," Kaos said, the trace of a smile tugging at his lips.

Evren's heart rose to see his spirits lifted, however slightly. Everything seemed suddenly turned on its head, as if, in entering Willardton, Kaos became a completely new man. The thrill of hope and possibility shot through Evren.

"In truth," Kaos said, "we might stay here for a few days, even a couple of weeks, perhaps. We need to raise funds for the next leg of our journey. There is a ship that can take us most of the way, instead of us having to row ourselves. Also, we will need food, other necessary provisions. I can hunt, sell meats and furs. And I have an old friend here, a blacksmith by the name of Darien. He may have some work for me as well. But first, we will stop at *Merella's* and finally get you some shoes."

He smiled down at her, and she replied with a grin.

"Thank you," she said. "You've done well, keeping my feet healed and as comfortable as they can be. But I am sure they will appreciate shoes as much as I will."

Kaos nodded and then picked up pace a little.

As they wound through town, Evren drank in every detail. If they were to stay here for a while, if she was to have the luxury of imagining that she had an actual home again, she wanted to memorize and enjoy everything about this place for as long as she could. They wove through cobble-stone streets lined with cottages and gardens and shops, through dirt streets lined with stables and humbler homes and a welding shop. Back onto a cobblestone lane lined with various shops, as well as people pushing carts and shouting their wares of spices, furs, silks, books—all manner of treasures. The people themselves—the Forest-footer Elves, Kaos answered when she asked—had skin fair as Evren's, with red, blonde, or brown hair that flowed in wild curls or waves. They seemed a friendly sort, most of them smiling or nodding in passing. They wore earthy tones, and their clothes looked practical but comfortable, loose tunics and dresses and thick boots. Above all, Evren especially adored their pointed ears.

As they scaled a hill, a glimmer of something caught Evren's attention. Between the cottages and trees dotting the hill that sloped down to their left, she glimpsed the ocean. Sunlight bedazzled its gentle waves with many multi-colored sparkles, making the ocean appear almost like a stretch of stars tangled in a nebula cloud.

"Here we are then," Kaos announced, just before stepping inside a two-story stone building shaded by more lofty trees. Evren glanced up and read the sign: "*Merella's Trade.*" She glanced inside the window, saw the fine dresses displayed there. Her heart cheered, for it had been a long age since anyone had taken her shopping, even if it was just for a practical pair of shoes. A lady could still look at things and dream, couldn't she? She wandered toward the window, entranced by one of the gowns, a long flowing one made of a shimmering white fabric. She wondered what the fabric would feel like between her fingers.

Then Kaos softly cleared his throat, and Evren looked up to see that he held the door open for her. A boy and girl laughed and scampered inside, a young woman trailing calmly behind and thanking Kaos. Evren hurried inside, and Kaos followed.

"Sorry," Evren said.

"It's all right," Kaos said, placing an arm around her and moving her to the side, out of the way as another family scurried in the door. "I am certain it's been some time since you were surrounded by such fine things—it has been a while for both of us. I am going to go speak with Merella, catch up with her a moment, hopefully sell some of the furs we've acquired. You look around and enjoy yourself."

Kaos gave her a final glance and nod, then walked over to the counter where a Forest-footer woman with a pretty face and graying blonde hair welcomed him with warm words and a handshake.

As the two chatted, Evren wandered about the store. Never had so many fine things surrounded her—not just in a while, as Kaos had guessed. Even back home, they had no shops carrying such a vast array of every kind of ware one could imagine.

There was a whole shelf filled with spices; the boy and girl who had run inside earlier tried to reach the spices, saying they wanted to smell each one. Evren pulled down each jar for them, and together the three of them enjoyed the sweet aromas, wrinkling their noses and laughing at the bitter, more unpleasant ones.

There were fruits, dried meats, and fresh breads for sale. Small animals in cages, birds and cats and dogs. Figurines carved from wood, others from glass, and intricately painted. Clocks and compasses and other mechanics. An array of fabrics, yarns, and wools. Dresses and tunics crafted in many styles that Evren had never before seen. She supposed that was the benefit of living in a seaside town—getting to trade with and experience many new things from many kingdoms across the ocean.

Evren made her way at last to the dress she had seen on display. The sun shone through the window, bedazzling the white fabric just as it had the ocean, making her think once more of stars—or of snow. Ah, how long since she had witnessed a good snow! The Rozul had said their winters got cold but that it rarely snowed there or any of the other islands, unless one traveled farther north. As Kaos was intent on the south, the idea of seeing snow again any time soon seemed a feeble hope.

But Evren was content. Content to enjoy this seaside town with him. And content to run her hands along the fabric of the white dress. It flowed through her fingers with all the warmth and softness of starlight itself. She placed it to her cheek, savoring its touch.

"Evren?"

Evren jerked from her reverie with a gasp and turned toward Kaos who stood smiling, a sort of mischievous twinkle in his eyes. A large, bulky leather bag was slung over his shoulder.

"Ready to find some shoes?"

"Oh! Yes. I had nearly forgotten."

"That much, I can see. Come."

He led her toward the back of the store. There awaited several narrow shelves filled with shoes and boots of many shapes, sizes, and colors.

"I know you are drawn to pretty things," Kaos said. "But I think for now, a practical pair of boots should do. Something comfortable and sturdy for the road."

"I would be content with whatever you are willing to give me," Evren said. "I may like looking at pretty things, but I don't need them. My sunstone is enough, and that more for sentimental reasons than anything." She touched the gemstone at her heart.

Kaos nodded. "Good. We are on the same page then. Have a seat. I will find something for you to try on. If the size is wrong but the style fits, we can always have a pair tailored."

He drew over a stool and Evren took her seat. Kaos examined the shelves closely, narrowing his gaze in a scrutinizing fashion. Then, he drew down three pairs of boots, each with a certain feminine touch but certainly durable enough for a hard journey.

After some debate, the two of them settled on a pair made of a soft brown leather. Evren's feet felt like queens inside their comfort, and Kaos said they were thick and strong enough to withstand several years of hard travel. As they intended only a couple more months' journey, the boots would be more than sufficient to do the trick.

After the boots, Kaos led her over to a wall lined with cloaks; more cloaks hung on wracks nearby.

"It *is* warmer in the south, but the nights can get quite cold," he said. "There is no sense in my having a cloak while abandoning your own needs. Go ahead and select one. Whichever you like."

"Are you sure?" Evren asked.

"I can afford it. And even if I couldn't, Merella is gracious and knows I will pay my dues before we leave Willardton. Go ahead; we won't leave here till you pick one."

He gave her a mock-scolding look. Evren smiled, happy to see him playful for once. Not wishing to discourage the mood, she set about searching through the cloaks.

There were many fine cloaks from which to choose. Some made of velvet, others with satin linings or bits of lace. Red cloaks, white ones, blue and purple ones. Kaos had said to choose whichever she pleased. In the end, she secured a thick, soft, dark green cloak to match his both in color and in warmth.

Her new treasures in tow, Evren followed Kaos toward the counter where the two of them took their place in the small line of customers that had formed.

As they waited, a small voice piped:

"Excuse me—sir—are you a knight?"

Evren's attention drew to the small blonde boy standing beside Kaos and staring up at him; it was the boy Evren had helped earlier with the spices. Kaos turned this way and that before thinking to look down for the source of the small, excited voice. The boy's eyes gleamed expectantly at Kaos.

Kaos knelt, smiled at the boy, and said, "I am indeed."

"And that's your sword?" The boy pointed.

Kaos nodded. "It is." He drew the blade and set it across his lap. The boy's eyes widened then glanced at Kaos with question. Kaos nodded, and ever so carefully, the boy ran his fingertips across the sword's smooth, flat jasper.

"It's a *real* sword?"

Kaos laughed lightly. "It is."

"And you're a real knight?"

"You tell me. What does it take to become a real knight?"

The boy twisted his face into a pensive frown. After pondering some moments, his eyes lit up again and he said, "A dragon! Have you ever fought a real live dragon?"

Kaos' smile faltered. His entire body tensed, and for a few moments he sat so still, Evren wondered if the boy's words had somehow turned him to stone.

Then, at last, he rose to his feet, sheathed the sword, and said quietly, "I have. I have seen and fought a dragon in my time."

The boy stared, wide-eyed and wondering. Evren stared with the same new awe.

"Do you think *I* can become a knight one day?" the boy asked. "A real knight like you, with a real sword?"

"What is your name?"

"Turlough, sir. But I am called 'Terry.'"

Kaos smiled down at the boy once more. This smile was more serious, troubled by whatever memories talk of the dragon had triggered inside him; Evren could see clearly in his gaze his struggle to maintain composure. But he placed a hand on the boy's shoulder and said, "Young Master Terry, any man can be anything he desires, if he will only put his mind, determination, and hard work into becoming that thing."

The boy continued to stare at Kaos with steady admiration. Kaos glanced away, looking uncomfortable. The boy's glance wandered too, to rest upon Evren.

"I heard that all knights have a fair maiden they fight for. Is *she* your fair maiden?" He pointed at Evren.

"No," Kaos said quietly. "She is my...my..."

Evren's heart fell a little with Kaos' usual harsh honesty, especially after the wonderful day they were sharing. Then again, she supposed it was good he kept them in check, reminded her of their true roles. Despite herself, she felt amused at how lost for words he suddenly seemed. She knelt down, smiled sweetly at the boy, and said, "His squire. I'm his squire."

"His squire?" A curious frown crossed his face. "But you're a girl..."

"Girls may be squires too, if they may be knights; you *have* heard of the Lozolian Echelon?"

The boy nodded.

"As I said: if *they* can invite girls into their fold, then *I* may become a knight as well."

Terry looked satisfied for a moment. Then, glancing her up and down, he frowned and said, "Where's your sword?"

Evren's smile widened; their little game somehow cheered her. "I'm rather a new squire. We haven't gotten quite that far yet in the training."

Terry looked pensive once more. After considering her words a few moments, he lifted his chin and declared, "I *am* going to be a knight someday. But I will have my own squire *and* a fair maiden. And they won't be the same people. Fair maidens shouldn't have to do all the work of a squire. They should be free to do maiden things." He gave Kaos a challenging glance before scampering off to rejoin his sister and mother across the store.

41

Evren rose to her feet with a laugh. "Is that your intention for me, Sir Jaspar? To make me run all your errands for you?"

"I asked you only to call me 'Kaos,'" he muttered, glancing away as if suddenly embarrassed. "And I am perfectly capable of running my own errands. You *are* a lady, whether mine or not. And I *shall* continue treating you as such."

As Kaos stepped forward to pay for their things, Evren's heart didn't know whether to laugh or cry, for she had the feeling his words were an exact declaration of how things would indeed continue for her: always a lady, yes, but with no chance of breaking through his many walls, claiming the heart she knew still beat deep within, and becoming *his* lady.

Upon exiting the store, Kaos announced they would head then to *Lord Jay's Inn* to wash up, eat supper, and rest from their travels.

"We'll stay at the Inn as long as we're in Loz," Kaos explained. "The Inn is run by a friend of mine. His name is 'Kaspar,' but most people call him 'Lord Jay' or simply 'Jay,' a favorite nickname that goes way back. Jay has been like a brother to me for many years. He will give us comfortable lodgings for cheap."

Evren walked silently beside Kaos, soaking up not only his words, but the layout of the town and especially the brilliance of the sun dazzling on the ocean below. The sun had dipped low since they had begun their shopping excursion. The great blazing star now fell halfway below the horizon, setting the sky afire with bright pinks, oranges, and golds, and just a splash of purple. Stars began to dance in the purple. All this magnificence reflected in the waters, colliding heaven and earth in such a way that it seemed an entire separate universe was reflected on the water's surface.

They turned a bend and left their view of the ocean behind. Up and up they climbed, between thick trees and past more houses, till at last, they came to a two-story building made of sturdy stone. A sign over the door declared in fancy letters that they had arrived at *Lord Jay's Inn for Weary Travelers*.

One Starry Knight

Evren followed Kaos inside the inn, immediately glad for the scents of rich foods wafting through the spacious, airy dining room. Men and women chatted and laughed gaily around wooden tables. A long counter stretched along one wall where men sat on stools, talking and drinking; one man sang to the music of a nearby fiddler, slurring his words and stumbling about.

Several men prepared and served drinks behind the counter. As Kaos led Evren over to the bar, he seemed to focus his attention on one man in particular. Stopping at the far end of the counter, Kaos leaned casually across, watching the young man with dark skin like his. The man sported many long, thin black braids pulled back and tied with twine. He hurried about to refill drinks, always with a bright smile and sometimes with a joke or two. Only when one of the other men nudged him and nodded in Kaos' direction did he look up. His eyes met Kaos' and widened. Then, with a grin and a whoop, he set down the bottle in his hand, ran toward Kaos, and propelled himself artfully right over the counter, landing on the other side with all the grace of a cat.

"Kaos! My dear brother!" He threw his arms around Kaos and clapped him on the back.

Kaos returned the embrace with a wide grin. "It is good to see you, Jay. It's been too long."

"Truly," Jay said. "I never thought to see *you* again. At least, not in these parts, or any time soon. What brings you here?"

"The Lady Evren and I," Kaos motioned to her.

Evren smiled and nodded at Jay, all the while taking note of the pendant hanging on a silver chain about his neck. The pendant was an oddly shaped stone colored with bands of black, white, and silver; it looked almost akin to the hilt of Kaos' sword.

"We're just passing through," Kaos added. "We're headed south." He gave Jay a meaning look.

"*Oh*," Jay said. He glanced with sudden curiosity between Kaos and Evren, then back again. His gaze lingered with question upon Kaos, but when it appeared Kaos meant to give no answers, Jay brightened with a smile again, his eyes dancing, and he said, "Well, please do have a seat. I will get you some food to refresh you. And a drink or two for you, Kaos—I swear we've the best beer in from Arabis. And a sweet Labrinian wine for the lady, perhaps. And I trust you'll need a room for the night as well?"

"Several nights," Kaos said, "if all works out. I need time to secure funds for the last leg of our journey. Is Darien still in town?"

Jay nodded. "Yes. And he will indeed be pleased to see you—perhaps even more so than *I* am, especially if you are willing to run his errands for him. His last apprentice recently set off to start his own trade. But go ahead, make yourselves comfortable. Actually—perhaps you'd like to wash up first? Come. I'll take you to your room at once then."

Jay danced his way across the room. Kaos and Evren hurried to keep up as he turned into a short corridor then leapt lithely up a tall flight of stairs. At the top, Jay led them down a long hall flanked by doors. At the fourth door on the left, he stopped, knocked, and then opened it and motioned Kaos and Evren inside.

"One of my finest rooms. Nice and airy, with space enough for you *and* the lady, Kaos. I hope it suits your needs."

"Anything safe and warm and dry will suit our needs in the coming days," Kaos said. With another smile at his friend, he extended his hand, and Jay grasped it warmly. "Thank you," Kaos added. "I will discuss payment with you later this evening—"

Jay raised his free hand to silence him. "Don't worry about it. Get some rest tonight. We can talk business tomorrow. Or the day after if need be. Or the day after that. I'm not worried about it; you're a man of your word who always pays his dues. I am happy to help you and glad to have you here until the two of you are ready to continue...*south*, you did say?" His eyes flashed sharp curiosity.

Kaos' smile faltered as he said, "South...yes, south."

Jay turned his inquiring gaze to Evren once more. He studied her closely, and Evren began to feel uncomfortable. What was he searching for? What did he know about Kaos and the south that she did not?

At last, Jay broke his own trance and gave Kaos a polite smile. "I'll let the two of you rest now. Shall I have supper sent up? Would you prefer that?"

Kaos nodded stiffly, suddenly his old, withdrawn self once more. "Yes. Yes, that would suit us well. Thank you, Jay."

Jay nodded at Kaos, then at Evren a final time. "My pleasure, and a good evening to the both of you." With that, he sped from the hall and down the steps as quickly as he had come.

Evren stared after him in amusement. "He is...That was quite the leap he took over the bar. He's very graceful for such a solid-built man."

Kaos nodded. "He served alongside me once in Carmenna. He too was a knight, for a time. But before that, a dancer. He's always possessed a flare for the arts." Kaos stepped inside the doorway of their room and motioned Evren inside. "After you, milady."

Evren's heart staggered, as her feet would have done, had she been walking already. She stared at Kaos a moment, then hurried past him, not wanting to risk the smile bursting inside her to bubble to the surface and make him realize the importance of the endearing term. The last thing she wanted was to make him withdraw from her again as he had in their past several days of traveling.

As soon as Evren had recovered, she paused to glance about the room and take in the surroundings of her new, if temporary, home with a sudden glee that allowed her to release her smile after all. A single large bed with soft, clean, white linens. A writing desk, small wardrobe, and chest made of polished red wood. A screen set in one corner for dressing. Two large windows that allowed what remained of the setting sun's rich, red-orange glow to cast a warm sheen across the cozy room. Evren moved further into the room and found a small fireplace, currently unlit, and an adjoining room with a lavatory and a tub for washing.

Evren leaned inside the small washroom, which was illuminated with the warm orange glow of an oil lamp. She admired the deep tub and imagined what it might be like to soak deep beneath hot, steaming waters scented with soothing oils. Her grandmother had prepared such baths for her as a child before they had grown poorer and had to make do with lye soap. Even then, the hot waters had always refreshed, seeming to cleanse Evren from the inside out. The hotter the better. Her grandmother had always teased that she must be a fire demon born from the stars themselves to be able to withstand such hot temperatures.

"Do our quarters meet with your approval?"

Evren nodded.

"Would you like to be the first to wash up?"

Suddenly feeling Kaos behind her, she glanced over her shoulder and up at him.

"I *am* eager to wash up. But if you would prefer to go first, I'm sure you were traveling long before I joined you."

"And I am still certain it's been longer for *you*, between the two of us, since you had a proper bath—or a proper meal for that matter. We'll soon fix both. Come. I'll show you how to work the shower."

"Shower?"

Kaos brushed past her and walked over to the tub. He pulled a cord dangling over the tub. After several tugs, water began to gush out from a hole set far up the wall, cascading into the tub like a small waterfall. Evren watched in amazement, and Kaos grinned, looking pleased.

47

"Jay spares no expense. There's a bit of rubber in that corner there that will plug up this hole..." He pointed inside the tub. "That's the drain. Plug it to make the water stay inside. It'll be hot; it's heated from the ovens below. And it's fresh, comes straight from the lake nearby. Go on, give it a try."

He held the cord in one hand and motioned her over with his other.

Evren walked over. The space was small, and she positioned herself carefully so as not to step on Kaos' toes. She leaned forward to take the

cord in her hand, but as she grabbed it, she stumbled, nearly toppling into the tub. Kaos caught and steadied her. Then, positioning her so that she was steadied by his strong frame behind her, he placed his arms around her and guided her hands to the cord.

Together, they pulled, and a greater stream of water than before spurted out, splashing them. Evren released the cord in surprise, laughing and falling back against Kaos who laughed too. Evren let herself lean back then, enjoying the warmth of his body and their sudden closeness. The small space seemed even smaller, but rather than feeling suffocated, she felt freer next to him, in a way that meant comfort and safety. He rested his hands on her shoulders, slid them down her arms, took her hands in his. Evren leaned her head back just enough to realize how close their faces were, despite his resting a head taller than hers. She could easily turn, take his face into her hands, lean up on her toes, and kiss him...

Kaos gently slid his hands from hers and moved her to the side so that he could slip from the small space. He paused in the doorway without looking at her and said, "I will leave you to your privacy. There are robes on the hook there. I will leave your clothes behind the changing screen for when you are done washing. You'll have privacy to get dressed while I take a bath myself—leave the water for me, please. No need to draw more and waste it." He glanced up at her then, and Evren shivered at the intensity of his gaze. She ached at the sudden distance between them and longed to run to him and bridge the gap once more. What could possibly go wrong if she did? What could possibly go *right* instead?

But the way he watched her also unnerved her. He was a man, and she just a girl who knew little about men—save one, and that was long ago. She was the first to timidly break their gaze. The next moment, she regretted her fear and glanced up again, but he had already gone and shut the door behind him.

Evren found the rounded piece of rubber Kaos had spoken of and plugged the drain. Then she drew her bath, adding a few drops of oils from the nearby shelf. When sweet scents and the healing balm of steam permeated the room and filled her lungs, she carefully undressed and slipped beneath the hot waters.

Easing down into the bath made her body keenly aware of its aches and pains from their journey. But before long, the water and oils soothed those pains, especially those of her tired feet.

Evren enjoyed a few minutes in the bath. Then, not wishing to take up too much time and make the water grow cold for Kaos' turn, she set about scrubbing every inch of her skin and rewashed her hair several times until she felt the filth of their trek sufficiently washed away.

Upon finishing her bath, she found two towels made of fresh white linen hanging on the wall Kaos had indicated, along with two robes. Once dried and dressed, she stepped back inside the main room of their dwelling quarters.

Kaos seemed to have vanished for the moment, though he had lit an oil lamp on the desk before doing so. Evren took the chance to hurry behind the dressing screen. A dress had been slung over it, and Evren started to take it in her hands but then froze, taken aback. This dress felt clean. Her own dress still lay on the floor next to the tub, wrinkled, soiled, and torn. Evren took the dress before her down and inspected it. Clean, sturdy cloth, perfect stitching. This gown was akin to hers, plain and practical, but brand new.

Evren prepared to slip the dress over her head when some movement made her glance up. She fell back against the wall in shock at the sight before her. For a moment, she had thought another woman hid behind the screen with her. But then she saw the freshly washed glass gleaming in what remained of the setting sun's glow and crept closer, staring. She stretched forth a hand and delicately touched the glass. Many months had passed since she had viewed herself in a mirror. Her red-gold waves of hair had grown longer, wilder. Her figure was thin, her skin pale as ice. Her long nails were jagged and chipped, like a wild beast's claws. The only feature that could be considered "pretty" at the least were her eyes. She looked like some wild fairy or other woodland imp from one of her grandmother's tales. Perhaps *this* was why Kaos could not love her?

She shook the idea aside. He was not so shallow. She finished drying herself then pulled her dress over her head and tugged it down and around her petite frame.

Stepping from behind the screen, she noticed the bathroom door was closed and heard some movement from within. Kaos must have sneaked in while she was getting dressed.

She wandered over to the window and stared out at the darkening sky. Nightfall had nearly completed its black painting speckled with so many stars over the peaceful seaside town. Only the palest light remained along the fringes of horizon visible between houses and trees. A few people moved in the streets below, but most had retired for the evening.

Evren turned her gaze upward. A clear night, perfect for stargazing. Lamplight in the streets below dimmed the stars' brilliance a bit, but Evren's keen eyes caught sight of every one of them, her familiar friends.

A knock on the door drew Evren's attention in that direction. She walked over and opened it to see a young man with wild blonde curls holding a wooden tray. The tray held two bowls steaming with a thick,

delectable-looking stew, some raspberries, fresh bread, and water, along with a mug of beer and a smaller, more elegant mug with a red liquid Evren assumed was wine.

"Thank you," she said, taking the tray into her hands.

The young man said nothing, only stared at her.

"Do you need anything else?" Evren asked. "Sir Jaspar is busy at present, but when he comes out, he can pay you…"

"No!" the young man said, snapping from whatever reverie. "Sorry, milady. No. There is nothing. Can I get anything else for *you?*"

Evren shook her head. "No, thank you."

"Then I bid you good night, milady."

"Good night. And thanks again."

The young man bowed then hurried down the hall and down the stairs.

Evren brought the tray inside and kicked the door closed. She set the tray on the desk and eased onto the edge of the bed, watching the food and suddenly realizing her intense hunger. Finally, she turned away, not wishing to tempt herself. It would be disrespectful to eat without Kaos— and besides, in sharing a meal with him, she could further imagine this airy, quaint hotel room to be their true home.

After a few minutes, Kaos emerged from the bathroom in his robe, toting both his and her dirty clothes which he threw in the bottom of the wardrobe. Gathering some fresh clothes from the leather sack he had obtained on their shopping trip, he glanced up at her and said, "You can eat, if you like."

"I'll wait for you."

He nodded. "Suit yourself," he said, then disappeared behind the screen.

Once finished, he was clad handsomely in a royal blue tunic, new breaches, and new boots. The blue perfectly accented his dark skin. Evren found herself gaping a bit and looked away, grabbing the tray to occupy her hands and saying, "Where shall we eat?"

Kaos shrugged and sat on the edge of the bed with her. "Just set the tray between us, and we'll manage."

Evren set the drinks on the desk, placed the tray on the bed between them, and passed a bowl of stew to Kaos. He broke the bread and gave her the bigger half.

They ate in silence. The warm bread melted in Evren's mouth, and the stew quickly filled the hole in her belly. When their meal was nearly done, she tried the wine. She flinched at its sour taste, but then its magic went quickly to her head, making her feel just a bit bolder than usual. She secretly wished she'd had a bit of wine earlier, in the washroom with him. But she would use the liquid courage now in what ways she could.

"So, you like children?" she asked, savoring the raspberries. "You seemed to, with the boy in the store."

Kaos nodded, wiping the rest of the stew from his bowl with his bread and taking a bite. "I do. I value their innocence, their sense of wonder of the world. Sometimes I wish I could return to that way of thinking and being."

"Perhaps we cannot regain innocence; knowledge steals that from us. But Amiel forgives all who ask, and so we *can* decide to start over again, with a pure life..."

"In the south. The south will help both of us begin again."

Evren reached out and took the larger mug into her hands. She extended it toward him with a questioning look. He studied her, seemingly amused, and said, "You seem changed this evening. Is tonight your first time having a drink?"

She nodded.

He took the mug from her. "Thank you." He lifted it toward her. After a moment, she took the hint and touched her mug with his. Together, they drank. Evren smiled, a little less shy than usual at the close way he watched her.

Evren studied him closely in turn. Head to toe. Her gaze lingered on the scars etched up and down his arms. The thick, long scars mapped across his dark skin as if some wild beast or skilled swordsman had met their mark many a time. She reached out and touched them. He tensed, but when he did not withdraw, she began tracing her fingertips along the scars. Gradually, his rigidity melted, until, for once, he seemed to feel comfortable at her touch.

"Where did you get them?" she asked quietly.

Kaos tensed again. Evren continued to trace the scars but wished she had left her curiosities to herself—especially once he pulled his arm away and muttered, "In the north. I got them in the north. One of many reasons for abandoning it for the south…"

"And there are other reasons?" When he did not reply, she ventured another question that had been on her mind for some time, "Who is she? The woman you keep thinking of? The reason you will not love me or anyone else?"

Kaos stared at her, clearly startled. He stared for a long moment, and Evren wondered if her question had stolen from him all ability or desire to answer.

Then, at last, a fierceness masked his face, pulling it once more into a solemn frown. "You are, indeed, a most perceptive young woman. But my heart was not broken. So do not think to fix it. It was ripped out and cast on the side of the road to beat alone for all eternity."

Then what if, she thought to herself, *I sought first to find it and* **then** *fix it?*

Kaos rose from the bed.

"I am going out tonight." He flung his cloak over his shoulders. "To the pub, to have a few drinks, catch up with old comrades. I might stop by the blacksmith's as well, to see if Darien will have any work for me." He secured his sheath with his sword about his waist. "If you need anything, Jay can assist you. If he's not downstairs, he's on our floor, last door on the right."

Stooping down, Kaos fished about in his leather satchel.

"Here," he said, holding a small woven box toward her. "These are for you."

"For me?" Evren said. Her brows rose, and her heart leapt as she inched forward on the bed and took the box into her hands. "A surprise?" She glanced up at him with question.

Kaos nodded toward her and granted a small smile. "Nothing lavish or extraordinary. But go ahead and open it."

Evren removed the lid and glanced inside. At the sight of the ripe red fruits, she laughed in delight.

"Strawberries—you remembered." She smiled up at him. "Thank you."

"How could I forget? It's hardly all we ate on the voyage down here."

"Thank you—oh!" She ran her hands down the length of her new dress. "Thank you for this as well. It's warm and in much better condition than my last."

Kaos nodded. "It fits you well."

His gaze lingered on her a moment more. Then, he walked over to the door, opened it, and said, "I will likely be out late. Good night."

"Good night," she said, but he had already left and shut the door behind him.

Evren sat on the bed for some time, savoring the strawberries and contemplating what next to do. Whether from the wine or Kaos' absence or the excitement of being in a new place, she felt far more awake than she expected she *should* feel after completing such a long journey.

She decided at last on setting about making herself more presentable. Perhaps true love wasn't built upon the state of one's outer appearance, but whether Kaos could ever love her or not, she cared about him and wanted to look as nice for him as possible. She couldn't fill out her bony, willowy figure overnight. But she could do other things to begin transforming herself into the honorable lady she felt suddenly capable of re-becoming in Willardton.

Finding a bit of wood that had splintered off from one of the baseboards, she filed her nails until they were as smooth as she could get them. Then, she dug about Kaos' satchel until she'd procured a pocketknife. Using the mirror behind the dressing screen as a guide, she cut a few hopeless knots from her hair, trimmed it just a bit, then braided and tied it back with a bit of cord to prevent its getting further tangled.

Once satisfied inasmuch as she could be with her appearance, Evren looked around the room to see what else she could do. Spotting Kaos' old tunic in the wardrobe, she wandered over, sniffed it—and recoiled with a gasp. She hadn't noticed the stench during their travels, likely because she had smelled just as repulsive. Now that she'd been lathered in fine oils, the scents of sweat, animal's blood, dirt, and adventure itself overwhelmed her.

Carefully taking the tunic and her old dress and slinging both over one arm, she left their room and hurried down the steps. She just prepared to venture out into the night when a voice stopped her:

"Whoa, hang on. Evren, is it? Wait. Please."

Evren glanced up. Jay had called to her from behind the bar counter. All customers had since seemed to vanish to their homes for the evening, or perhaps to their rooms upstairs for those who were lodging. Jay stood wiping off a glass, all the while staring at her with a concerned frown.

"May I ask where you are going?"

"Just out to do some laundry. Is there a lake nearby?"

Jay shook his head. "I promised I'd keep an eye on you. Kaos wouldn't like you going out like this."

It was Evren's turn to frown. "I *know* there's a lake nearby because Kaos mentioned one being used for the baths here. But if you won't help me, I'll simply take his things down to the ocean, which is quite a ways down the hill. If it takes me longer, or if I get lost before he returns..."

"All right then, all right…" Jay released a great sigh. "This is why I didn't want this job. Kaos knows what a pushover I am for helping pretty ladies like yourself. If you go out the door there and around back, up the hill and into the woods, there's a lake not far in. Just make sure you're back before *he* is, all right? If you can do this, I promise not to breathe a word. You should still have about an hour, but I wouldn't push things past then."

"How do you know how long he'll be out?" Evren asked. "Did he used to stay here and conduct business with the blacksmith quite often?"

"The blacksmith?" Jay's face wrinkled in confusion.

"Yes. Kaos said something about running errands for a blacksmith— Darien. I assume that might be the business he's about right now—"

"Oh!" Jay's face brightened with recognition. "Yes, Darien. Yes. Kaos lived in Willardton for a time, a little while back. He is well-known enough in these parts. But run along. I don't wish to see either of us in trouble. Kaos has a big heart—but his temper can be just as big, if given cause."

Evren didn't need to be told twice. She had seen the flare of self-righteous anger in Kaos' eyes that day he had bought her in the slave market, the way his hand had constantly hovered over his sword as he had loathed Master Brant. She didn't wish to ignite that same anger in him— most of all, she didn't wish to ignite the same worry she had also seen in him that day. He had spent much to save her and bring her to safety. She would not disrespect such a gift.

"I will be back in time," she said. "I promise."

Jay still looked uncertain but nodded and said, "Very well. I won't stop you—not that I suppose I *could*, even if I tried…"

Evren thanked him a final time then stole from the hotel.

Night's fresh, cool breeze rushed over her, filling her lungs, refreshing and making her feel even more alive with a spirit of adventure. Willardton was a wellspring of new chances for her. And for Kaos. And for possibly the two of them together. Temporary or no, she would make the most of their stay here.

She hurried behind the hotel and up the hill into the woods as Jay had said. Sure enough, after traveling only a short way into the woods, she happened upon a clearing with a large lake. Several row boats were docked, tied by thick ropes to the surrounding trees. Someone had left their linens to dry on the sprawling branches of a fallen tree. Fireflies danced over the lake, twinkling along with the stars reflected in the crystal-clear water's surface.

Evren knelt by the shore and scrubbed the soiled tunic and gown as best she could, wishing all the while that she had brought some of the oils from the washroom. She scouted the land around her till she found some herbs she knew were helpful for cleaning stains and freshening fabrics. Finding a rock and small strip of wood, she created a sort of mortar and pestle and crushed the herbs. As she rubbed them into the fabric, the dirt worked itself out till most had disappeared. Once she was as satisfied as she could be, she gave the clothes a final wash and returned with them to the hotel.

Back in hers and Kaos' room, she slung the clothes over the tub to dry. Maybe Kaos would think she had washed them in the tub, though if he asked, she would tell the truth; she had always made a horrible liar, despite her story-telling skills.

Evren climbed onto the huge bed then and sank gratefully beneath the thick covers. Softness and warmth enveloped her. She began to doze in and out of sleep. Snatches of dreams and daydreams merged, visions of her and Kaos gazing at the stars, then flying through them, of his taking her into his arms and dancing with her on the ocean shore, before stopping to kiss her passionately...

The door creaked open, jerking Evren from her dreaming, though she was too cozy to rise and greet Kaos. He would expect her to be asleep anyway.

Kaos released a deep sigh and set something on the desk with a kerplunk and a jingle-jangle that told Evren he had returned with a small sum of money. Footprints sounded dully as he moved across the room. Fabric swooshed as he removed his cloak and hung it in the wardrobe. A thud as he kicked off his boots, quieter footsteps as he walked toward the bed. Evren held very still and drew her breathing to a slow, steady rhythm.

The bed sank with Kaos' weight as he climbed in beside her. Evren felt something warm touch the top of her head and nearly flinched but stopped herself when she realized it was his hand. His hand rested there, on the top of her head, in a tender sort of way. Then, he let go, rolled over, and had fallen asleep in a matter of moments, snoring deeply.

This smallest token of affection lit Evren's heart with a hopeful new flame. Maybe it was nothing at all. Maybe it was simply some expression of his satisfaction at a successful night working and making a few coins for their trip. Whatever the cause, Evren fell asleep with a smile on her lips and a hope in her heart that perhaps she could, after all, someday become Sir Kaos Jaspar's "fair maiden."

The next night, upon his return, he stroked her hair.

The night after that, he kissed her cheek.

The third night, he held her, though only for few moments. Evren couldn't help sinking against him then. Perhaps he had realized she was awake, or perhaps her reciprocation made him realize he was breaking his own vow to himself never to hold her. At any rate, upon releasing her, he had still kissed her cheek before turning over and falling asleep.

These subtle touches gave Evren such joy that, whenever Kaos was absent, she spent her free time doing all she could to be helpful to him. She began to hope, and with hope came imagination and motivation. By day, when he was out hunting and selling furs or doing favors for Darien the blacksmith, she would tidy the hotel room, dust, take laundry down to the lake, polish his boots.

Kaos gave her a few coins to do with as she pleased; she bought some yarn and old knitting needles at the market and made a scarf. They had been in town long enough so that she had thoroughly explored it and met many of the Forest-footers, and one of the shopkeepers, Miss Bevin, was looking for someone skilled in knitting and crocheting; the winter season approached, and such items as scarves and hats would be needed. Evren's grandmother had taught her the craft of knitting; she would use it now to help hers and Kaos' purpose to reach the south.

Some days, Evren stretched her work out as much as she could, so that, once Kaos left on his mysterious nighttime quests, she would have something to occupy her till his return. Sometimes she would try to sleep, but until he had returned and his warmth nestled close to her, sleep was impossible. There was also the anticipation of his good-night kiss, which became a sort of secret ritual between the two of them. It was the greatest token of affection he ever afforded her, one she would not waste by sleeping through it.

Finally, one evening, her curiosities about his nightly ritual evolved into a great restlessness which soon overtook her entire spirit. She didn't even bother feigning sleep but instead stayed up, knitting furiously. Kaos found her that way upon returning from his day's work. At first, he tried to settle into bed and lay down beside her, but after a short while he got up and paced.

"Aren't you getting tired?" he asked.

"No," Evren said, keeping her gaze fixated on her work. "I want to finish this. Miss Bevin said she is eager to sell my work in her shop as soon as she can. And I am eager to pull my weight in this quest. If the only useful thing I can do is sell my knitting before we set off again..."

"That's not the only useful thing you do," Kaos said, a surprising tenderness in his voice.

"Is that so?" Evren said, finishing her row of knitting before finally glancing up at him.

His body language was tense, and he rocked on his feet, as if eager to be free from the confines of their room—it no longer seemed so spacious, after living there some days now—but a tenderness touched his eyes, and he smiled a little. "Yes, that's exactly so. In all my days, I don't think there ever was another time my tunic smelled so consistently fresh and my boots shone with almost the same brilliance as your sunstone. You take good care of me."

"The least I can do in return for you taking care of me."

Kaos' smile dipped a little into one of his pensive frowns. "I think you spoil me, actually. Even all this knitting...I intended you to use the money I gave you for yourself."

"I did," Evren said, lifting her chin. "I rather enjoy knitting, thank you. If you want me to have something pretty, you should have gotten it for me yourself."

Kaos looked taken aback for a moment. Evren wondered if she had overstepped her bounds but quietly returned to her knitting.

"I have to go out for an extra errand," he said at last. "I may be a while, so there is no need to wait up for me. Sweet dreams, and I will see you in the morning."

"Thank you. Good night."

Kaos pulled on his boots and cloak and hurried from the room.

Evren froze still and listened. Listened to his footsteps falling softly on the stairs. Listened as they receded altogether, filling her ears with a complete hush.

Springing from the bed with a burst of energy, Evren laid her knitting aside, unable to compose a single loop more, and zipped over to the window. She watched him walk away from the hotel and head deeper into town. She flew from the room and down the stairs, pausing to glance into the dining room. Jay stood at his usual post behind the bar, laughing heartily along with three other men. Evren glided across the room. Only as she slipped through the door and shut it quietly behind her did she realize it wouldn't have mattered had Jay seen her. He had watched her go out to do laundry or take a walk many a time late at night. Perhaps the daring of tonight's outing had gone to her head for a moment, making it seem more forbidden than usual.

The streets were empty save for a random passerby here and there. Evren broke into a fast run, feeling almost as though she was flying as she hurtled herself in the direction she had seen Kaos go. She began to worry she had lost track of him—after all, he had seemed in rather a hurry—but then, as she threw herself around a corner, she spotted the edge of a cloak disappearing around a bend. Less keen eyes would not have detected such a small detail. But hers did, and the fabric was definitely the same as that of Kaos' cloak.

Evren sped silently toward the building where he had turned and paused to peek around its stone wall. Sure enough, Kaos hurried down the street. The cobblestones had ended, replaced with dirt paths. Good. It would be easier for her to follow quietly that way.

Evren followed Kaos via a clever game of hide and seek, ducking behind houses, shops, and trees every few seconds, peeking out, and then darting to the next hideout. The farther she went with him, the harder her heart drummed till she feared it might leap from her chest altogether. Just like their bedtime kiss, she felt like they were about to share another special secret. They usually only experienced this time of night separately, but now, they would experience it together. And, like the kiss, Kaos wouldn't know, but she would. And that meant more than enough to her. As soon as they reached their destination, she would learn the source of his lifted spirits these past days, the reason he had dared to show a bit of affection to her. Perhaps—whatever it was—perhaps it was something else she could help him with.

The buildings grew sparser, the trees more frequent and closely knit. Shadows blanketed their path, providing a natural cover from the starlight and moonlight so that Evren dared to move a little faster.

She began to wonder if they would ever reach their destination when at last, Kaos slowed his pace. A small group of houses huddled together, including a few built in the trees. A blacksmith's shop rested on the left side of the lane; Evren expected Kaos to turn there, thinking perhaps he went to see his friend.

Instead, he turned and entered the building on his right. A tall structure, three stories high, built of weathered stone. Lights shone from some of the windows. Silky curtains fluttered in the soft night breeze. The sign over the door read *Senga's Paradise* and showed a picture of a pretty barmaid holding a large glass of beer. Strange—it looked similar to the hotel they were staying at, if a bit fancier. Perhaps Kaos had a friend passing through and had come to visit him or her.

Laughter and the clanking of beer mugs echoed from within. Evren glanced about to see if anyone was around. Then, stealing from her hideout beside a lofty tree, she crept over to one of the first-floor windows and peered inside. The window was open, and the silky curtains fluttered back to reveal a large dining room and bar like Jay's. Several men sat at the bar while two men behind the bar chatted gaily with them, serving drinks. Off to the side, a large group of men sat around a large, round table, eating and drinking. Pretty women young and old sat on their laps, some with their arms around their necks, some kissing them. The women were dressed head to toe in pretty gowns that shimmered. Evren wished she had such a gown. Maybe then Kaos would look at her the way these jolly men looked at their ladies.

Kaos' voice jerked her attention to the far side of the room where he spoke to a middle-aged Forest-footer man with graying curly hair. The man handed something to Kaos who then began his ascent upstairs.

Evren darted back to the great tree and jumped up. It took several attempts before she had grabbed the lowest branch, but from there she pulled herself up and scrambled up the tree till she was eye level with the second floor. The only lit window was far to her right and she strained to see, but upon catching a glimpse of Kaos and hearing his footsteps continue to echo, she guessed he was heading for the third floor and continued her ascent till she was level with it. Then, ducking safely behind the branches, she parted them and peered out.

At first, nothing. Several windows were lit, but no movement stirred within them. Perhaps he had gone to one of the rooms on the other side of the building. If he didn't show soon, she might need to switch trees...

Then, something moved in one of the windows. Someone—a woman—had stood up. The woman had been so still, Evren hadn't even noticed her sitting so close to the window. Now she disappeared further into her room. A lock clicked; a door creaked open. Soft laughter. Footsteps. The woman reappeared, with someone beside her. The breeze blew the curtains back to reveal a thin yet curvy figure with porcelain skin and clad in the same pretty silks as the maidens downstairs. Her hair fell in long waves of strawberry blonde. Her eyes shone green as emeralds, and her cheeks were red with the wine inside the glass she held with one hand. With the other hand, she pulled the someone further inside the room, toward the window. The curtains closed, then fluttered open again—and suddenly Kaos was taking the woman into his arms, setting her wine glass aside, and kissing her. He unlaced her dress and slipped it down over her narrow shoulders. As it fell to the floor, revealing a flawless body beneath, Evren's heart fell with it.

This. This was the source of his happiness in coming to Willardton. Every bit of affection he had shared with her had been a lie, a mere aftertaste from being with his lover.

The soft orange light dimmed inside the room and then extinguished. Evren tore away, clambered down from the tree, and raced blindly back into town. All she could see was Kaos kissing the red-headed woman. She needed to purge that image and all the emotions wanting to accompany it from her mind. She needed her thoughts to get lost anywhere, anywhere at all, far away from the swift downward spiral they attempted to suck her inside.

She ran hard, not once stopping or slowing, till she came to the lake where she always washed his clothes—*his* clothes—and found one of the row boats docked there. Unwinding the rope, she jumped in and pushed off from the shore. She rowed hard until the boat rested in the middle of the lake. Then, at last, she stopped, lay down, and stared up at the stars.

Evren stared for a long time. She recited the constellations, the stars that comprised them, the names of their nearest brothers and sisters. She gazed far beyond what human eyes could see into the hundreds of thousands of stars beyond, into their prismatic nebulae and diamond clusters. She floated far beyond the stars, to her old home where the stars were sacred and revered as guardians over all living creatures. But no matter how hard she looked or how far she imagined, she couldn't lose herself in them. They had lost their magic, and she didn't know how to reclaim it. She was just a girl in a boat floating on a lake and staring at a universe far vaster and more significant than she ever was or could be. Because another woman was far more significant than her right now to the man that she...

Before the word could enter her mind, tears escaped her eyes. She quickly blinked them away, forced them back. *She must not.* She must not cry, any more than she must allow herself to think that singular word and the overwhelming rush of feeling and lack of control that would accompany it. She could not hate him, much as she wanted to in that moment. But she must not love him either—or at least, she must not acknowledge her sudden fear that she was beginning to love him far more than she had ever thought she would dare. She must rebuild the walls around her heart—when had they fallen, and how had she failed to notice?—and stop this love dead in its tracks before it was too late.

It's already too late, her heart mocked. *You fell for him the moment he first showed you the stars.*

Shut up, she pleaded. *You don't know anything. Anything at all. You bring only pain. I won't let you this time. I won't let you do this to me...*

Evren sat up, rowed the boat back to shore. She secured it tightly to the dock. Then, she wandered back to their hotel. She stole inside, granted Jay the ritual smile and nod; as far as she knew, he hadn't spoken a word to Kaos of her midnight adventures, and she did not wish to give him reason to start worrying now.

She dragged herself up into their room and threw herself on the bed. There, in the stillness, wrapped in blankets but devoid of his warmth, there most of all, she wanted to cry. But she must not. To cry was to feel things for him that he would never feel for her.

Curling up into a ball, as if hoping to squeeze the pain right out of her, she closed her eyes and told herself to go to sleep. She didn't want to feel his gentle kiss on her skin when he returned. She didn't want his false comfort and sweetness. It too had lost its magic, their secret bedtime ritual...

But sleep would not come. For a part of her knew his good night kiss was not entirely false. He gave it in secret, and thus he gave it for himself—it must mean something to *him*. Maybe it didn't mean what she wanted it to mean, the same thing it meant to her. But it must mean *something*.

Evren didn't know if she told herself this because it was true or because she wanted it to be. All she knew was that, as the door creaked open, the feel of his kiss and of his warmth settling into bed beside her still comforted her, whether she wanted it to or not, and that he alone was the tonic she needed to slip at last into a dreamless sleep.

6

Evren's heart bled each night Kaos went to his lover, but she stayed the pain each time, using denial as her tourniquet. After all, she and Kaos had never shared a romantic understanding. If anything, Kaos had made the opposite perfectly clear.

Their routine continued as before. Kaos ran his errands by day to secure funds for the next leg of their trip. Evren stayed back to tend to the hotel room, though she began taking her knitting outside more often, down by the lake or under one of her favorite trees just at the edge of the wood. Before, tending the hotel room had been like taking care of their home. Now, after her late-night discovery, she wasn't sure if her heart could still afford to continue pretending this guise. The four walls of their room seemed to suffocate at times, demanding she step outside for fresh air and perspective.

Then the rainy season dawned. Winter was coming, the Forest-footers said. It always started with a chilled breeze and steady rain. Evren was stuck inside for a couple of days.

Evren focused solely on her work, knitting several scarves and hats. Miss Bevin had been more than pleased with her work and had begun selling it already, turning quite a nice profit for both ladies.

One evening, the rain had finally quieted when Kaos breezed into their room, his gait more upbeat than usual. A brightness, almost like a smile, lit his eyes. Since that morning, he had changed from the usual blue to a deep crimson—another brand-new tunic, by the look of it. Like the blue, the blood red nicely accentuated his dark skin, though Evren thought she preferred the blue. She studied him curiously a few moments before returning her attention to her work.

"Sorry I missed supper tonight," Kaos said. "But Darien had some extra errands for me to run, and I was eager to assist. We've saved almost enough to complete the rest of our journey south, I think. A little extra for food and other provisions, and we'll be able to head out. Just a few more days here, I promise."

"You make it sound like I've only been enduring," Evren said. "I rather like it here. It's far more a home than I ever had in Rozul. The people here are kind."

"They are. And this is indeed one of the happiest places I have ever known. But we'll find an even brighter future in the south. But for now— I noticed you've seemed a little downcast these past couple of days. So, I got you something at the market on my way home. Something to cheer you up, I hope..."

Home, he called this place. A painful longing tugged at her heartstrings. Despite herself, curiosity also tugged at them and she glanced up at him. Another glance at the bed, and she noted the collection of packages sitting there.

"...but you have to close your eyes. And hold out your hands."

Evren studied him a moment more, intrigued by the playfulness in his voice. There was such a lightheartedness in his gaze that she could not help feeling a bit cheered. She closed her eyes.

The sound of rustling and ripping paper told her Kaos was opening one of the packages. He laid something in her lap. Evren clutched at its softness, warm and smooth as sunrays, light as air. Her heart jumped with excitement, and yet, it couldn't possibly...

"Go ahead," he said gently. "Open your eyes."

Then she opened her eyes, and it *was* possibly. She stared down at the white dress laid across her lap, shimmering in the lamplight.

"Do you like it? I saw you looking at when we first came into town, at our first stop by *Merella's*."

"I love it," Evren said quietly, running her fingers along the gown's silky softness. She had expected its sparkle to be tainted somehow, for her to think only of the women at the hotel—of the woman making love to the man she loved. And she did think of them, in their pretty dresses like this one. But she did not think *only* of them. The shimmering fabric made her think also of the stars, of looking at the stars that first night with Kaos. Though this bittersweet meaning clung to the dress' beauty, she would wear it and think of him as she did. After all, he had bought it for her. Like the secret good-night kisses, the dress had to mean...*something*.

"I have to run out again tonight," Kaos said. "Some late-night business. I won't be home till you are likely long asleep. No need to stay up for me."

He walked over to the mirror, straightened his cloak. Then, he hurried over to her and kissed her on the forehead. She didn't look up at him, her gaze fixated on the soft fabric running through her fingers, but then he touched her chin and brought it up so that her gaze met his. For a moment, her heart stopped inside her. They had never been so close, face to face—except for that time in the washroom—and he watched her with such a tenderness that, for the first time in many days, she wanted suddenly to kiss him.

"Pretty red-head," he said softly. "Sweet dreams."

Then, with a final lingering glance, he stole from the room.

Evren sat bewildered, as though the breath had been knocked clean out of her. A myriad of emotions flitted through her—joy, anger, elation, sadness, giddiness. None of these feelings matched up or made sense. None of them should be allowed to exist inside her heart in such close proximity, and she felt like she might burst from feeling them in such swift succession.

She jumped to her feet and did the only thing that *did* make sense in that moment.

She tried on the dress.

As she stood watching herself in the mirror, all other emotions fell away as she swelled instead with a strange admiration. The way the fabric hugged the curves of her thin frame perfectly, making it look almost attractive again. The way its snowy white accented her golden-red hair. The way its glisten reflected the sparkle of her sunstone, and the way the sunstone nestled perfectly in the V cutout along the neckline. The dress fit like it was made for her. Once again, Kaos' attention to detail was right on target.

Then why didn't he notice what should be most obvious? Why didn't he understand her feelings for him? Or, if he *did* see, why did he toy with her, buying her gifts in one breath and running off to his lover the next?

Evren stared at the mirror, at the dress, reminding herself over and over of his generosity. He had saved her. He took good care of her. He bought her fine things.

As she went through this mental checklist, it struck her, the common thread:

Surface level. Everything he gave her was surface level, whereas she had given him her heart. And this would have been bearable, at the least, except that she knew about his lover. She had to stay cooped up in this room every day, essentially playing the part of a sweet, innocent housewife, while he shared parts of himself with another that he would never, ever share with her. He had as good as said so, after all.

It wasn't fair.

It wasn't fair at all, and Evren determined to confront this injustice, if for no other reason than to make sense of it. Kaos was a closed book, like a sacred diary that someone had locked up before throwing away the key. If he wouldn't talk to Evren and make her understand things, then she would have to find answers for herself.

Throwing her cloak around her shoulders, Evren hurried downstairs. She didn't bother granting Jay the usual friendly nod and smile. Kaos had broken the façade of their little life together. She was no longer bound to upholding the façade herself.

As she scurried through the streets, Evren wondered what exactly she expected to do, once she got to the fancy hotel filled with men making love to their women in fancy gowns. She couldn't bear to see Kaos and his lover together again. Perhaps she could wait till he left, and then steal inside. Perhaps his lover would have answers that Kaos didn't, or that he refused to give.

Upon reaching *Senga's Paradise*, Evren scaled the great girth of a tree she had climbed that first night she'd followed him. She took extra care, realizing she had left in a great hurry in her new dress and not wishing to tear or get it dirty in the slightest.

At last, she crouched in the branches, poised in her hiding spot and peering out carefully at the window belonging to Kaos' lover. A gentle orange light glowed from within, as before. The curtains fluttered, allowing Evren a glimpse here and there of the red-haired woman as she moved about in her room. But Evren heard no voices, nor did she catch a glimpse of anyone else. The woman seemed alone. For a moment, Evren's heart rejoiced—and then it fell, just as swiftly and to much lower depths than before. Perhaps this simply meant Kaos was seeing a different lover tonight.

The very idea upset Evren beyond reason. She climbed down the tree and marched up to the hotel's front door. For a moment, she hesitated, still having no idea of what she was doing. Except that she was moving forward. Doing something was better than always doing and learning nothing. She opened the door and walked inside.

Once more, a hearty group joined in the bar area, drinking, laughing, talking merrily. Some of the women sat in their pretty dresses on the laps of their men, holding them, kissing them. Some glanced up curiously at Evren as she entered. Others glared and clung more tightly to their men. Some of the men stared at Evren with mild interest, others with unconcealed lust.

Evren ignored them all and walked up to the bar.

"Good evening, milady," the bar tender said.

"Don't call me that," Evren snapped, before she could think twice.

The bar tender looked as taken aback by Evren's boldness as she felt herself. But then he smiled and said, "As the lady wishes. And just what is such a lovely, spirited maiden as yourself doing in a place like this on this fine winter's eve?"

"I'm here to see my sister," Evren said, spinning her story quickly and hoping the pieces fell into place. "Third floor…"

"Ah, yes! You must be Mandy. She will be pleased to see you. She's been fancying your visit, though we didn't expect one for another few weeks or so. But the surprise will lift her spirits, as she's been a bit gloomy. I suppose you know where to go."

Evren nodded.

"Then go right on up. She took ill this evening; nothing catching, but she'll be free—not entertaining any customers at the moment."

The bar tender winked at her. Evren forced a polite smile and nod before turning and rushing up the stairs.

With each step she climbed, Evren's heart seemed to pound a little harder and race a little faster, spurring her feet to move faster as well. Only when she had reached the third floor and counted the doors to her right and found the one that should align with her tree did she stop short, catch her breath, and wonder:

What *was* she doing here? What did she hope to accomplish?

Kaos would be furious if he found out. She was breaking his trust.

But he had already broken hers.

But two wrongs didn't magically create a right.

But he hadn't broken her trust, because they weren't lovers…so she didn't break his trust in coming here.

But she did, because it was none of her business.

But she was already here. She lifted her hand and knocked on the door.

"Come in," a woman's voice called gently from within.

Evren's knock and the woman's beckoning words—together, they created a link to Kaos' world. They formed an irreversible catalyst, breaking down some of the wall Kaos had built between them. Any lingering anger rushed away from Evren's heart which raced instead with new possibility. There was no going back now. She must open the door, see what she could see, and learn what she could learn.

Evren opened the door, stepped inside, and stared. The woman sat up on her bed, drew her fine silken sheets up over her naked body, and stared back with the same bewilderment. At first, Evren thought she stared at her own reflection. Upon looking a little closer, Evren noted the shorter length of the woman's red-blonde hair, the slight upturn of her nose, the wrinkles hugging the corners of her eyes—subtle differences, ever so slight. At the least, the two of them really might have been sisters. No wonder the bar tender had so readily accepted her story.

"You must be Evren," the woman said. She reached for a robe on the bed. Turning away from Evren, she let the sheet slip down and donned the robe. "You may come in and shut the door."

Evren did so quietly.

"Come," the woman said, looking once more at Evren who noted the vivid green and familiar shape of her eyes. "I won't bite you, if you won't bite me—which I understand if you would..."

"No, it's not that way," Evren assured, hurrying over and joining the woman on the edge of the bed. "That is, I know he visits you here frequently. But I haven't come about that. I'm not angry at it. I only want answers. *Any* kind of answers."

"He doesn't talk to you?"

Evren shook her head. "No. No, he doesn't. Not a word."

The woman narrowed her gaze, not in an accusing way, but as though she studied Evren very deeply. Perhaps she too was enamored at the near reflection sitting before her, or perhaps she was simply deciphering how best to next answer.

"I know only a little. When a man is intimate with a woman for a long time, even a man like Kaos, he opens up to her in other ways, begins to trust her a little. I asked him once if he'd had any true lovers before me. There was a girl. A girl he loved very much. She died...But I'm afraid that's all he would tell."

Evren's heart had begun to lift, but now it sank inside her. She had guessed there might have been another girl. But the fact that she had died made everything seem so very final and hopeless. Her heart ached for Kaos, and she suddenly wished to be back at his side, to comfort him in whatever small way she could.

"Thank you," she said, granting the woman a small smile. "Thank you for telling me what you could. I know we are perfect strangers; you didn't have to reveal anything to me. I know Kaos would not be happy at my learning things this way, but he is so closed. Though, having learned what I have, I wonder now if I can ever see him happy. It breaks my heart to know he lost someone he loved so dearly..."

"You love him," the woman said, a gentle statement more than a question.

Evren's heartstrings tugged inside her, but she hushed their longing melody and said, "I haven't known him long or well enough to love him. I care for him very deeply. But he has made it very plain how he feels on the subject of love—and hence I do all in my power to guard against such feelings."

"But you *could*," the woman said, leaning forward a little, her voice growing to a yet gentler, quieter hush. "You *could* love him. You could love him very much indeed, if given the chance."

Evren nodded, ever so slowly, terrified to admit it to herself, let alone to this mutual confidante. "Yes...if I thought it could mean anything. You don't know...a part of me *has* wanted him to make love to me, as he does to you. But I know it could only ever mean something to *one* of us, and I fear that would cause me more pain than would be fair for either of us to bear."

The woman took Evren's hand. Her emerald eyes narrowed in a strange sort of pleading—perhaps "longing" was a more fitting term—and she whispered, "He would appear as the stones of these walls—thick, strong, unbreakable. He would want you to think of him this way. But do not fool yourself into believing he is an entirely impenetrable fortress." She hesitated; sadness flitted through her eyes and she held her breath, as if afraid to speak her next words. But then, with a resolved sort of smile, she sighed and said, "He *does* care for you, you know."

Evren stared at the woman. The faintest hope tried to flicker inside her heart, but she extinguished it. She didn't want to be told merely what she wanted to hear. She wanted to hear the truth...and for the truth to align with what she wanted to hear, if it could...even though it couldn't possibly. She must not allow herself to become distracted with such feelings of false hope...

"How would you know?" Evren asked at last. "Does he talk about me?"

The woman shook her head. "No, not really... But he *has* mentioned, and I can just...tell. I can tell in the way he looks at *me* now. There is a different kind of emptiness in his eyes than usual. He once fancied that I filled a void. But your coming, it creates a *new* void in him, whether he would recognize it or not. A void that you could just as easily fill if he would let you."

"Your assumptions are generous. But I told you already how steadfast he is. He says he has no heart. He says it with such conviction."

"But do you believe that?"

Evren almost answered that, yes, yes, she did. She believed it because she trusted him so perfectly.

And yet...

Actions spoke louder than words. She thought of strawberries, and of the dress she wore, and of starlit rides across the lake, of sharing the stars together and spinning endlessly into the heavens.

"No," she said quietly, fighting hard the emotions that wanted to pour forth; they hit against the tourniquet of her heart like a battering ram. "No, I don't. But I'm also uncertain I am the one who can find it. He started to open up when first we met…and then he closed and has remained even more closed since."

"Fear," the woman said. "Fear drives a man to do—or not do—strange things. People are cowards in the face of their own happiness. If you believe that he may be your happiness, then you may well be his too. Anything I would give to see the sadness leave his eyes for good, even to the point of giving up his company altogether. Pursue your happiness—yours *and* his."

"But he won't let me in," Evren said quietly. "He *won't* let me in. This," she motioned about the room, "this is as close to him as I have gotten. And I had to steal it."

The woman nodded. "Sometimes we must steal happiness, for ourselves—and for those who don't know better. He might not recognize what he has, in you, or what he *could* have, if he'd let himself. You don't seem like one to take the lead. But just this once, you might need to."

Just this once. The woman made it sound like the easiest task in the world. Expressing her heart to Kaos might be a singular task, but that, by no means, made it a light or simple one.

Evren stood to her feet. "Thank you. Thank you for telling me everything you could. But I should go now."

The woman nodded. "You should. He will be looking for you. And he *will* worry."

Evren stared, feeling her heart plummet inside her, this time from anxiousness rather than sadness. "What do you mean?"

"I sent him away this evening. Not because I am ill, but because, if I may make my own confession… I care about him as well. We are women, you and me. No matter our situation—harlot, prisoner, princess, damsel in distress—we fall in love with the men who care for us, in whatever ways. We form attachments. It was not in my heart to make love to him tonight when his eyes were filled with thoughts of another. He needs to be with you. Not me. If he won't recognize it, then I need to move on at least, for my own sake."

Evren's heart broke for the woman, for the brokenness visible beyond her gentle smile.

"We are more kindred spirits than I would have ever imagined in coming here," Evren said. "I *am* sorry..."

"Do not weep for me," the woman said. "I chose my fate long ago. And you can still choose yours. Go to him. Tell him you love him. But hurry. He will have made it back to your hotel by now. He'll have the entire city looking for you if he thinks something has happened to you—"

"Thank you again!" Evren said, flinging herself from the room and hurrying down the stairs. She rushed from the hotel, ignoring the bar tender as he shouted inquiries after her.

Evren sped through the town as fast as her feet and racing heart would take her. She glanced continuously at the stars, noting and cursing their subtle movements across the sky. For just this once, could not time stand still? Her grandmother had used to tell her a story, a fairy tale about a young maiden who must flee a castle before the strike of midnight to hide her secret from the prince she loved. Even so, Evren raced against time to share her secret with the chosen prince of her heart.

Finally, the hotel loomed into view. Evren swung the door open wide—

And fell right into Kaos' arms.

For a moment, he stood frozen still as she leaned against him, struggling to catch her breath and drinking in his scent at the same time. Then his arms closed around her and he held her, one hand on her waist, the other on her head, stroking her hair. For once, his reserve melted away. For once, they became almost one—

Then he took her by the shoulders, jerked her back, and gave her a hard glare, like a father scolding his child.

"Where the hell were you?" he demanded.

Evren stared back. Tears sprang up from her heart at the accusation in his gaze.

"I was only out. For a walk. I—I'm sorry…" She took a deep, shuddering breath and held it, hoping it would hold back the tears, but a few fell.

Kaos' expression softened a little, as did his grip on her shoulders. "I'm sorry too. If I frightened you. Come in, out of that cold air. We'll talk in our room." He placed an arm around her, drew her inside.

As they headed toward the stairs, Kaos called to Jay, "You were right. She's here. She's safe."

Jay glanced up from behind the bar where he stood drying dishes. He gave Evren a gentle smile, nod, and a wink, and then she and Kaos scaled the stairs.

Once inside their room, Kaos removed his cloak, and hers, and hung them in the wardrobe. Taking her hand, he led her to the bed and sat her down. He removed her boots, then his.

Finally, he released a great sigh, looked at her, and said, "You have no idea how worried I was about you. I would have had the entire city guard out looking for you, save that Jay told me to wait. He said these walks of yours are something of a routine, assured me you would be back soon…"

"I'm sorry," she said. "I often have trouble sleeping…"

…*when you're not here*, but her lips wouldn't free the words suffocating her heart.

"I don't want it to seem like I'm trying to cage you," Kaos said. "I don't want you to feel like a prisoner—like the life you came from before. I don't want you to ever feel that way again. I know you are a free spirit. I know you need your earth and trees and water and sky, the same as I do. But until we reach the south, we are not truly safe. I spoke with Jay, and I want you to stay in your room at night, from now on. Only two or three more days, and we should be able to set sail from here. And then, the last leg of our journey south. And then, in the south, safety. And you can have all the earth and water and sky that you want."

He cupped her face in his large but gentle hands, leaned down, and kissed her forehead. He sat beside her and drew her close, and she leaned her head on his shoulder. For the longest time, they sat that way, he with one arm around her, playing with her hair. It was the closest he had ever come to holding her, and it felt more right than anything had felt for Evren in the past several days—nay, the past several months.

His having a lover had changed everything. Then, Evren's talking to that lover had changed everything yet again, once more creating an entire new dynamic between her and Kaos. Evren had learned so much about him in the past hour that the past several days she had spent bewailing her love for him seemed suddenly an entire lifetime ago. She could hardly believe that she had been so childish and selfish instead of waiting to know and understand the truth.

After a time, Kaos laid back with her on the bed. She lay close to him, tracing the scars on his arm, and he covered her with their thick, warm blanket.

"You look beautiful, by the way," he said. "The dress suits you perfectly."

"Thank you..." she said, and she smiled. She had almost forgotten she was wearing it, with all that had transpired.

Her smile soon faded into a pensive frown. This time, as she traced his scars, she wondered if he had gotten them trying to save the woman he'd loved before—the one who had died. If so, how had it happened? Had his lady love perished by the sword, by flames, or some by dark magic? Who or what could possibly outmatch a force as determined as Sir Kaos Jaspar?

Even more so than these questions, another pressed at her heart.

"Kaos?"

"Yes?" He waited a few moments and then prompted, "Go ahead. Speak your mind."

Evren took a deep breath, opened her mouth—

And then closed it, her courage fleeing her as quickly as it had come.

As desperately as she wanted to speak her mind, fear froze the words inside her throat, lodging them there and choking her to the point of being rendered speechless. Once she asked him, if the answer was rejection, if he didn't feel anything for her at all, the rest of the magic that had already begun to wane between them would be lost forever. She wasn't ready. She wasn't ready for him to tell her "no." She needed to go on pretending just a little longer.

Tomorrow, she told herself, *tomorrow I will tell him how I feel…and ask him what, if anything, he feels for me.*

Evren snuggled as close to him as she dared, and while he still wouldn't wrap his arms around her, he for once let her rest her head upon his chest. She drifted to sleep that way, tracing the scars on his arm with one hand and clutching her sunstone with the other. If only she could use one of its wishes to make her feelings known. If only things could be that simple.

7

The next night, Kaos did not go to his lover but instead stayed in the hotel with Evren. She wondered if the red-haired woman had turned him away, feigning illness again. Then she wished she had gotten the woman's name; they had shared a connection, and it would have been nice to know her by more than her face and the secrets she had so kindly bestowed upon Evren. As the sun set, Evren and Kaos lay on the bed together. Evren lay on her stomach right beside Kaos, as close as he let her, tracing designs along the folds of the soft linens beneath them. She had woken not long ago from a nap, and he shortly after her.

As Evren's hand continued to move in circular patterns, Kaos asked gently, "What is it? What has troubled you these past days?"

Evren's gaze locked on the bed sheets, on their smooth and continuous white. Her heart beat wildly inside her. How she wished she had confessed her love last night, when the woman's words had lit her with the courage of new hope. Overnight, that courage seemed to have vanished altogether through the dark spell of so many doubts now assailing her. What if the woman was wrong? What if Kaos didn't care for her at all—or worse, if he loved her merely as some damsel in distress he was meant to save? What if paid heed to the things she enjoyed merely out of knightly duty? What if that's all she was to him—some task to carry out? Why should she even assume he could ever *want* to love her? She, this scrawny, awkward girl with her head in the clouds, when he could surely choose any woman she pleased...

Evren glanced up at him—and there her gaze remained transfixed as he stared down at her with such a tenderness in his gaze, such a concern. Whether because he had just awoken and sleepiness stripped away his guard, or whether he had peeled them away himself for once, the thick walls he always kept built between them were lowered. This was her chance. Now or never. And yet, she still didn't want to know. She didn't

want to break the bond that had formed between them, whatever it was, whatever it meant. Speaking her heart could mean creating a closer bond, yes. But it could also mean completely unraveling the one that already existed...

Realizing she was on the verge of tears, she blinked them back. She glanced away, taking a huge breath and feeling the weight of sadness pressing literally against her heart, making it difficult to breathe.

"Evren..."

Kaos touched her chin, drew her face up so that she had to look at him again. She blinked. Her tears fell. He cupped her cheek and brushed a tear away with his thumb. Her heart broke. It might break more if she told him. But she knew it would break most if she never did.

"Kaos...I know... I know about the other women."

Kaos stared down at her. Bewilderment flashed in his eyes, and then his face hardened with a somber frown. She couldn't tell if he was suddenly angry with her and wanted to bury herself beneath the covers and remember only the tender look he had given just moments ago.

Lowering his hands from her face to his lap, he said quietly, "Woman."

"But there used to be others."

"Yes. Yes...many others. But why are we having this talk? It should make no difference for us—we *did* agree..."

Evren stared at him, baffled for a moment. She saw the doubt flicker in his gaze. Kaos was no fool. He could not possibly believe for a second that the development of any feelings toward him were yet utterly impossible—he, the man who had rescued and cared for her, shown her the stars and brought her strawberries and pretty dresses.

"*You* agreed," she said. "*You* made the rules, for both of us. Why will you make love to them? All the city girls, but you will not even hold me?"

"You said you cannot make love *without* love. And so I do my part to respect that. I could make love to you—but I could not love you."

But I could pretend that you did, she thought. Though they lay so close to one another, the vast distance between them pressed an overwhelming ache against her heart. *Besides, it would mean something to* **me**. She had said before that she couldn't. But how quickly a woman can change her mind; once she actually falls in love and begins to admit it to herself, she would give everything to the one who has stolen her heart, without expecting anything in return.

"As for why I will not hold you," he said, "I think I made that plain enough the first night we met—equally as plain as you made yourself on the subject of intimacy. Holding someone is its own breed of intimacy. To me, it means that person belongs to me. But in reality, it always means that I feel things for them that they do not feel for me in turn."

"Do not presume to speak for me," she said. "Do not tell me how I feel toward you. Do not put those feelings in my heart, those words in my mouth..."

"What are you saying?" Kaos gave her a hard look.

"Kaos, I—"

The door burst open. Jay fell inside the room, doubled over and panting hard. Gasping for breath, he staggered against the door frame. Sweat drenched him and he looked as though he might pass out any moment.

Kaos sprang from the bed, rushing over and demanding, "Jay. What is it? What's going on?"

Jay drew a few more gasping breaths before they began to steady. He took a deep breath, then looked up at Kaos. Evren flinched at the wild fear blazing vehemently in his eyes, as if he had seen a whole host of ghosts resurrected and assailing him.

Kaos took a step back. He reached for his sword but then realized he didn't wear it and lowered his hand. His entire body grew rigid. Evren could almost imagine his hair bristling like that of a wild beast prepared to attack and defend its own.

"Jay, just tell me what the hell is going on—"

"He's here," Jay said bluntly. "He's looking for you. He's in the streets, raving like a madman. Threatening to torch the home of anyone who hides information about your whereabouts."

"How? How can he do this? Can't the guards stop him?"

"He...he has a power. A power I never saw him wield before. He's already cut down many of the guard. Some dark magic resides within his sword. A dark flame—"

Kaos whirled and darted toward the wardrobe, quickly donning his belt with his sheathed sword.

Evren jumped from the bed. "What do you need me to do?"

"Run." Kaos glanced up at her fiercely. "Run with me. We're leaving—now. Stay close to me. Run hard and fast and don't look back." He flung his cloak over his shoulders and cast hers in her direction. He threw her boots toward her before pulling his on. Evren quickly donned her cloak and boots, watching as Kaos grabbed several small pouches filled with coins and stuffed them inside his satchel. Then he hurried over to Evren, took her hand, and dragged her toward the door.

Jay fell back against the wall, out of their way.

Kaos paused to look at him and say, "Be safe, my friend. Get out of here. Get everyone to the cellar if you can. He won't find you there—"

The shrill sound of glass exploding rang in Evren's ears; a brilliant burst of orange and yellow light shot past, and Kaos yanked her to the side. The flames landed, setting the floor ablaze. Kaos pulled Evren after him while Jay began running down the hall, throwing doors open and commanding everyone to follow him. Men, women, and children streamed into the hall, fear shining visibly on their faces, some screaming, a baby crying. As Evren and Kaos prepared to dive down the stairs, she resisted him, digging her feet in and grabbing onto the corner of the wall.

"What the *hell* are you doing?" Kaos yelled, jerking her and making her release her hold on the wall. He took her by the shoulders and shook her hard, urgency blazing unbridled in his eyes. "We have got to go—!"

"We can't just leave them here to die!" Evren shouted back. "You're a knight—it's your duty to protect them—!"

"I am! He wants me, Evren; he wants me, and he'll want you. And he'll want us both dead—"

"Who? Who is this man who has you so filled with terror—?"

"I don't have time to explain! We must go. *I will not let him harm you*—"

"I am only one person. And these people are as innocent as I. Protecting them is far more important than sparing me—"

"***Not to me***!" Kaos roared.

Evren stared at him. Stared as the walls between them once more crumbled, more fully this time so that she saw clearly the desperation burning in his gaze. He was terrified to lose her. In whatever way, he did care for her. Her heart broke inside her once more. Why must his confession come now, amid such peril?

As the Forest-footers hurried down the stairs, pushing and falling against each other, Evren's heart broke for them too—especially the little girl being carried by her mother, staring back at Evren with tears shining in her round blue eyes. Evren had seen a corpse. She had seen how, in the blink of an eye, a body could turn from a vessel of life and light for a soul into an empty shell as that light extinguished and that soul vanished. She couldn't imagine that fate for the little girl staring up at her, almost pleadingly, as if she knew what was coming. She couldn't imagine this fate for any of them, the people who had become like her own in the short but precious days they had stayed here.

"Kaos, we can't—"

Kaos hefted her in his arms and threw her over his shoulder. She fought him, beating her fists on his back. She couldn't kick for he held her legs so tightly it hurt. She soon resigned herself as he pushed past the throngs swarming down the stairs. They passed a window on their descent; streamers of fire flew past outside, arching through the sky and cascading like falling stars—a false picture of beauty. Evren watched as one of the embers landed, setting fire to one of the cottages, and her tears fell with the flames.

Kaos burst outside the hotel and stumbled to a halt, nearly falling over. For a moment, he stood frozen still. Evren strained to turn around and see what he saw, what held him in such horror as to make him pause their urgent flight to safety. Then, he darted forward again, into the midst of the chaos surrounding them, and she saw too well.

Fire raged from every rooftop and tree, consuming everything. Forest-footers ran and screamed for the woods. A man rushed from his house, caught on fire and shrieking. He dove and rolled on the earth, putting out the flames, but then lay too still. Children cried. Mothers carried them, clinging to them for dear life. Several men with swords rushed toward the direction of the balls of flame streaking through the sky. The flames mimicked falling stars in such a shameful way that Evren was suddenly filled with her own angry fire. Perhaps Kaos would not save the Forest-footers. Perhaps he *could* not. Perhaps neither of them could spare the town from being destroyed. But she would not let them all die. She grabbed the sunstone at her heart and held it tightly.

Kaos turned down one of the cobblestone roads, heading in the opposite direction of the flames arching overhead. He ran hard and fast, clutching Evren tightly in one arm and drawing his sword with the other. Evren didn't fight him anymore. She simply held tight to her sunstone, watched the town, glanced upon each and every frightened face rushing past them, and concentrated hard.

They wound through the town and delved into the woods. Kaos took them deep, deep inside the trees, till at last they emerged into a small clearing at the crest of a hill. Kaos paused, turned, and stared down the hill at the blazing town below. Willardton had become a solid sheet of glowing orange, gold, and ruby embers.

At last, Kaos set Evren on her feet. She leaned against him, still holding her gem tight, still focusing.

Then he began to tremble head to toe. She looked up, and he was crying. She wanted to comfort him, but she must return her gaze to Willardton and the fire. She must remain focused for as long as necessary.

"I understand if you can't forgive me," Kaos said quietly. "I doubt I can forgive myself; we lingered far too long in Willardton. But I couldn't have forgiven myself either had he taken you or worse..."

Evren remained silent a few moments more. Then, upon feeling her magic completed, the spell sealed, she released a great sigh and allowed herself to fall against him. Still watching the fire, she leaned her head on his shoulder and placed a hand tenderly on his chest, right over his heart, which thundered wildly inside him. The sky flooded with color as the sun continued to set. It just crept beneath the horizon, lighting the ocean with pinks and reds, as though the Forest-footers' blood had been spilt after all and now stained the waters...

Evren shook the terrible image aside, for it was not true, nor would it be.

"There is nothing to forgive. They will be safe. No more lives will be lost this night."

"What do you mean?" Kaos began. Then, slipping his arms around her and holding her close, he whispered, "You made a wish, didn't you?"

Evren nodded against his chest.

"Was it your last?"

"No," she said quietly. "It will be my last when the gem's light goes out. Though I would gladly have used my last wish for them. I love them. I loved being there. Pretending that I had a home again..."

"I loved it too," Kaos said. "Too much."

He held her a moment more. Evren sank against him, treasuring his touch while wishing it didn't accompany the nightmarish vision of their beloved town destroyed before them.

"Come," Kaos said, turning her away from the heart-breaking sight. "We need to get back into the woods, under cover. We need to hide, and from there, plan how we will proceed. Once he realizes we are not in Willardton, he will keep searching for us. We must not be found, or their sacrifice is in vain."

Kaos and Evren dove down into the trees. They descended the other side of the hill, going down and down until Evren wondered if they meant to burrow into the very earth itself and hide themselves there.

They wandered till they found a stream that opened into a wide river. They followed the water, going against its currents and wading in the shallows so that they left no footprints. They traveled this way a long while, until night had settled over them. A little way further, another tree-laden hill stretched up before them, and in its side, the mouth of a cave opened. Roots twisted down from its ceiling. Bright green moss covered its sides. Insects skittered to and fro.

As they ducked inside, Evren inhaled the rich scent of earth and wished that Kaos had brought her to such a magical little place in happier times. They delved deep inside till the starlight and moonlight just barely stretched to them and the sound of the river rushing over stones had diminished to a hushed, lulling whisper. Then Kaos removed his sword and sheath and sat; Evren sat beside him.

For a while, they sat in silence. Kaos stared out toward the mouth of the cave. The woods were barely distinguishable this far back, but Evren felt that he gazed far beyond them.

"What now?" she asked after a time. "What do we do now?"

Kaos inhaled deeply and released his breath in a long sigh. "South. We still go south."

Evren hesitated to ask her next question. But then she remembered the way he had held her and saw the defeated slump of his shoulders. The stubborn hardness had vanished from his gaze, and she knew that the walls between them had been broken for good this time.

"Will you finally tell me what is south?" she asked. "Does it have to do with your scars? With the woman that you loved and was lost to you?"

Kaos glanced at her. Surprise flickered in his gaze, but mostly, pain.

"Yes," he said. "Yes, there was a woman I loved. In Carmenna, my home kingdom. I first met her when I had just begun my training as a knight. I had always thought to become a blacksmith, but I had my mother and sisters to care for, and being a knight meant better pay and the hope of someday attaining titles and wealth for them. Besides that, it seemed an honorable profession. Everyone encouraged me into it, till I fancied that I could, by some miracle, someday become a nobleman.

"The girl, my first love... She was daughter to a blacksmith—Darien, the same blacksmith I served while you and I stayed in Willardton. Her name was Amata. In my eyes, she was a Carmennan goddess. No one had ever been more beautiful to me, and I don't speak merely of her outer appearance. She had the most beautiful, pure spirit, full of this...this *joy*, the likes of which most people never come close to achieving..."

His voice trailed. For a moment, he looked as though he had strayed into a dream. He had begun to smile with remembering her, but now his smile vanished into a great, weary sorrow. Evren's heart ached with this sudden reminder that she could never fully fill his void, no matter what solace she might bring him. It ached even more at the pain etched so deeply on his face. If only she had power to erase such pain.

"What happened to her?" she asked quietly.

Kaos breathed deeply again. He looked as though he mentally prepared himself for a great battle.

Finally, he continued, "When I served in Carmenna as a knight, when I first started training, there were four of us—me and Jay, Codyn and Kamon. We all became sworn brothers to one another and loved each other as much as any blood brothers would. We were every bit as loyal, devoted, and true.

97

"Codyn and I had grown up together, played together all throughout our boyhood. We weren't born of noble blood, but we determined to work hard to become knights of Carmenna, and we did.

"Codyn gained much power during the Second Age of Dragons. He found a young dragon abandoned in the woods, thought to tame and control it. At first, they seemed a strong pair, a good pair. But then Codyn sought to gain power and favor with those who would use the dragons only for their own gain.

"Codyn also loved Amata. He had always been in love with her, from the moment he saw her. The three of us had been good friends, and he had seemed to accept our courtship. But with his new power, he thought he could sway her heart. He begged her to marry him, and begging soon turned to threats. I knew Amata was in danger. I took her and fled with her south. We ended up in Willardton for a time.

"When Codyn turned against me, he turned against Jay and Kamon as well, though his wrath for me was ever greatest. Jay fled to Willardton and started over with a simple life, starting his business at the inn. Kamon, however, escaped us most of all. For a while, no one heard from him.

"Then, word reached Jay, and he shared with me that Kamon had taken a lover on an island deep in the south. She was a magic mage with a special power in Sealing, a rare and protective magic. She had been using it for many long years to seal herself inside her island, making it so that no physical harm or illness could touch her. She loved Kamon enough to bring him inside her protective circle with her; by bestowing this gift to another soul, she reduces the years of her own life.

"I wrote to Kamon, begging him that if he would not take me, he at least convinced his lover to take Amata under their protection. Kamon didn't write back, but his lover did, inviting both of us. She said any family of Kamon's was akin to her and well worth protecting. She also sent a map to the island, which was cleverly hidden in the south. Amata and I began our journey south at once.

"But it was too late. Codyn and his dragon had already caught up with us. I did my best to save her. Codyn and I were dueling, and the dragon stepped in to defend its master…and Amata stepped in to defend *me*… Her screams still fill my nightmares…

"I was filled with nothing but rage the moment I saw the light leave her eyes. Not even my pain could reach me. I still hardly remember killing the dragon, it was such a blur. I just know that I did.

"Codyn claimed to have loved his dragon with as much devotion as I'd loved Amata. We have been sworn enemies ever since. He has been chasing me, and I have been running—not away from him, but to lead him away from my family. Because I honestly don't know if he would stop at seeing just *me* dead, if given the chance.

"But I run also because as much as I hate what he did to me, what he did to Amata, he is still my sworn brother. He was once my closest friend, and I still love him. I am loathed to kill him, and should he find me, that would be my only choice—be killed or kill him. I am a fighter, but not a killer. I have never once killed for sport or glory. Only to protect.

"Now though…it seems I may have little choice. I thought I had destroyed all the dragon scales but one—the one that could not be destroyed in flame. I sold it in Rozul; its powers are ancient, precious few would know how to use its magic. I received a large sum for it; it's the reason I could afford to buy you. But Codyn must have salvaged one of the scales as well, and now he is using it to power his sword…"

"Don't you think he still needs to be stopped?" Evren asked gently. "Do you really think he will stop using his power to destroy others just because we're safe where he can't find us? Do you really think he will stop looking once we reach the south?"

"No," Kaos said solemnly. "No, I do not. Now that he has this new power, that *does* change things. It may well be necessary for me to confront him. For me to slay him…or to be slain, if it happens that way… But I will take you south first. He doesn't yet know you exist, nor does he need to."

Evren moved a little closer to Kaos. Ever so gently, she slipped one of her hands into one of his and, with her free hand, once more traced the scars etched across his thick, muscle-lined arms.

"Is that why you close your heart to love?" she whispered. "Because of Amata? You're afraid to get attached to anyone else, to love them and lose them too?"

Kaos stiffened at her words but did not yet draw away—nor did he answer her, though his silence was answer enough.

"Before I was sold to the slave market," Evren said, "I too loved someone. His name was Baris. We were meant to be married. But then he grew very sick. The only way I could afford the cure was to end up where I did, with Master Brant. That was long ago and far away. I am sure by now he has found another wife, and even if he hasn't, there is no chance of our being reunited.

"I thought I would swear myself against love after that. In a way, I did. There *was* another young man I told myself I fell in love with. I used to watch him from my window in my cell as a slave, the same window I would watch the stars from. He had a cart that he sold fish, oysters, other sea foods from. I would watch the way he talked to the ladies, charmed them with his friendly smile, the sparkle in his eyes. The way his body moved so fluidly, almost like a dance. Once, when I was on my way to the slave market, we caught one another's gaze, the young man and I—and instantly, I fancied that every single smile or glance he had ever given the others had really been meant for *me*. I imagined an entire romance for us...

"I did that with others too. I think it was a means of survival through all those hard months. But putting up walls, indulging in fantasies...though it helped at the time, it was a hindrance later. We say it's to protect ourselves, to keep out the pain. But walls don't just keep out this or that. In keeping the pain out, we also wall ourselves away from seeing anything that might be really *good* for us too..."

Her voice trailed as she suddenly realized how freely she spoke. She half expected to look up and find that Kaos had moved away from her. But though their hands no longer touched, he remained close and watched her intently, seeming to absorb her every word.

"Where do we go from here?" she asked. "I know you say we will continue south. But if Codyn is still in Loz, there is a good chance he may find us."

"Loz is a huge island," Kaos said. "And though he may have gotten away with destroying Willardton, his story will spread, and the Echelon will soon enough hear of it and put a stop to it. He knew he could find me in Willardton because he had found me there before. I don't think he will be so foolish as to go razing other towns to the ground. But he *will* be looking for us, yes. I don't know if he ever knew my plans to travel south with Amata. But we can't take that risk. We will travel back north and set sail from the coast there. We might have to sail out of our way, but once we're on the ocean, we're safer—unless the dragon scale granted him powers of flight as well, but I doubt that."

"Do you think Kamon and his wife will welcome me?" Evren asked. "They don't know me..."

"No. They likely don't know of Amata's death either. They don't know many things. But I must trust that when we find them, they will welcome us into their fold. Or *you*, at the least."

"I won't stay there without you. You're running so hard to find this magical place of protection, when you forget my own powers." She touched the sunstone gem. "You are safer with me than with anyone."

"But your wishes are limited; isn't that what you told me?"

Evren was silent. Kaos nodded, seeming to accept her silence as all the answer he needed.

"How will we get there?" Evren asked. "You mentioned a map—I haven't seen you with one, not once. I don't doubt you being able to find the way for us; I am only curious..."

"The map was destroyed when I fought Codyn's dragon. But I had already memorized its every twist, turn, river, stream, its every tree and wrinkle and edge... I know the way well. My memory may try to hide many things, but it could never forget the way south."

A silence passed between them. A heavy silence of sadness and the ghosts of memories long wished forgotten. But as they watched one another, Evren thought it was also a silence of understanding. In the past few minutes, they had opened up to one another and created a suddenly strong bond that had perhaps existed from the moment they'd first met, but had just been waiting all this time to be discovered.

"Come," Kaos said, rising to his feet. "We'll move in a little further. It will be very dark, but I think you will like it..."

He offered his hand and helped Evren to her feet. His arm slipped around her shoulder, steadying her as they ventured further into the black depths of the cave.

They trekked until darkness nearly consumed them. Then, a bit further, a light shimmered. As they drew closer, Evren marveled at the way it shone and sparkled, creating patches of soft white along the cave's walls and floor.

Finally, Kaos brought them to a halt and whispered in her ear, "Look up."

Evren looked up and drew in her breath. A large fissure had been rent in the ceiling overhead, a jagged crescent moon shape that made the sky perfectly visible and allowed starlight and moonlight to shimmer through. Because they were so far from town, away from any other source of light, the stars bedazzled the sky with as great a brilliance as the first time they had watched them on the boat together.

As Evren continued to watch the stars, soothed by them, she felt Kaos' warmth as he wrapped his arms around her from behind and held her close to him. Brushing her hair to one side, he kissed her neck. His hold was strong and secure, yet his touch was ever so tender. Evren shivered. Her heart raced to what seemed twice its speed, and her mind spun so that it seemed the stars above them spun too, as if she and Kaos were in the boat all over again as on that first night, spinning and spinning, dancing round and round.

Gently, Kaos touched her cheek and drew her face to his. Their faces hovered close. Evren drew a shuddering breath, preparing for the plunge and yet feeling so surreal, uncertain it would actually happen. Perhaps this moment was a dream. She couldn't possibly be standing here, so close to kissing the man she loved, the man who had walled himself so carefully from her every attempt at affection. But then she thought, if it *was* a dream, it was *her* dream, and anything a person desired might happen in dreams. She turned to face him fully. He held her tight with one arm, his free hand at the back of her neck and running his fingers through her hair. Then she leaned up, and he leaned in, and their kiss was sealed at last.

Fireworks ignited inside Evren's palpitating heart, her fluttering stomach, her reeling mind. She knew only him, and kissing him, and him holding her. She clutched him to her, wishing they could be somehow even closer to one another. He kissed and held her with the same fervent passion, as if releasing all the pain and frustration he had shared with her that night.

For a moment, he broke from the kiss, leaving her stunned and breathless. He slung his cloak from around his shoulders and laid it on the ground. Then, he swept her into his arms, kissed her again. She wrapped her arms around his neck. He knelt on the ground and laid her gently on the cloak, cradling her head and kissing her still as he lay beside her.

As Kaos broke their kiss again, moving down to kiss her neck and shoulders, Evren opened her eyes and stared up at the stars shining down on them. They seemed to twinkle with the same heightened energy and light illuminating Evren's heart. Then, afraid to ruin the dream or wake herself from it, she closed her eyes once more.

They kissed for what seemed an eternity. At certain moments, Kaos would let his hands massage their way up toward her thighs or touch her breasts. His every touch electrified, so attentive and purposeful and pulsing with her same desire. But then he would pull back, sometimes with an almost frustrated sigh.

At last, Evren took his face in her hands, drew him back from their kiss, and said, "Kaos."

He looked down at her. "Yes? Is something wrong? Do you want me to stop?"

"No. No, I don't want you to stop, that's not it. I want…"

Her voice trailed as her heart thundered, imagining the words her voice could not utter.

He read the meaning clearly in her eyes and stared down at her with surprise. "Evren. Are you certain? I admit I want to. Your beauty is enchanting, and it's been long since I was with a woman I truly cared about. But you said once you could be only with a man who loved you as you love him."

"And *you* said you would not hold a woman who didn't love you," Evren said. "But you *know* that I love you, Kaos. I hardly know what's happening tonight, or if it's even real. But things are much changed between us. I haven't felt so close to anyone in such a long time. I want to feel even closer to you if I can..."

Kaos smiled down at her, a haunted sadness mixed with tenderness in his gaze. He stroked her hair, kissed her forehead. "You asked if I was afraid to love again because of me, because I am afraid of getting hurt again. I *am* afraid, but not just for myself—I'm afraid to hurt someone else. Afraid of hurting *you*."

"You don't have to protect me," Evren said, gently but firmly. "I am not some delicate, fragile being in need of protection. I break my own heart well enough in choosing to love someone who may never love me back. There is little you could do to cause me even greater pain...except perhaps continuing to deny me even the smallest chance..."

Pain deepened both the sadness and tenderness in Kaos' eyes. "I do love you, Evren. I just...I don't know if I could ever love you as much, or in the same way, that you so clearly love me. Your loyalty and blind devotion...I'm not the great hero you hail me as, though I can see the story of my past hasn't changed your mind on that. I can't promise if we do this that it will change things, or that we will be together forever. The future has never been set for me. Ever since Amata, I have attached myself to no one and nothing. I have purposely chosen no set fate for myself..."

"I know," Evren said quietly. "And I know I said before that it mattered, for you to feel the same way...but maybe it doesn't. I couldn't protect myself as a slave. I couldn't stop what they did to me. I vowed never to make love again unless I was absolutely certain it was to the man I would spend the rest of my life with—and I had never counted on that happening anyway, after losing Baris. But in reality...though I have been afraid to admit it...I would have let you make love to me the first time I realized I loved you. Because really, I think all I have wanted is to be able to be that close, to feel that again, with someone I love. Our feelings are open now. You know my heart. You don't have to love me in the same way. Only love me."

Kaos held her a little closer but still gazed down at her with question, warring with himself. Evren settled his dispute by drawing his face to hers and kissing him again. At first, he hesitated. Then, he released all inhibitions, allowing her same passionate fire to consume him, to consume both of them, as they, if but for a single night, became one with each other and with the stars rejoicing above them.

8

The morning after they made love, Kaos woke Evren with the dawn. They kissed for a little while before Kaos whispered that they must leave for sake of safety; he hadn't intended them to sleep so late. Last night had been their singular reprieve, but now they must continue their journey south until the south at last was reached. And that meant fulfilling their plan of finding Loz's northern shore and setting sail from there as quickly as possible.

Evren peeled herself from Kaos' arms, and together they dressed. As she drew on her white gown, its glisten no longer as brilliant with the taint of dirt and smoke from last night's flight, she glanced up through the crescent moon split above them. The rising sun lit the heavens with a deep crimson hue, like blood spreading across the sky. Evren was suddenly eager to leave the dream of the cave behind and be on the road again.

Ten days more they traveled, immersing themselves in the darkest depths of the forest, wading through shallow rivers to conceal their footprints and scents, slipping through narrow cave passageways. The going was far tougher than when they had made their way to Willardton, for Kaos was determined to take them by the most hidden, unexpected paths. More than ever, Evren was grateful for her thick boots, warm cloak, and Kaos' constant patience and guidance. She was grateful too for her keen eyesight whenever darkness fell; he led by day but relied heavily on her by night.

At last, as the sun set on the tenth eve of their journey, they emerged from the thick of the woods to a brighter patch where the trees were no longer so close-knit as to choke one another and any source of light, and from there they emerged onto the island's border. A wide stretch of white sand led to the ocean whose waves roared mightily, rolling and beckoning them to sail into the sunset's rainbow hues dancing upon its waves, and in that magical scene find refuge and escape.

Kaos gazed up and down the shore with a serious frown. Evren shivered and drew her cloak about her shoulders, all the while gulping in the fresh saltwater air, letting it fill her lungs and soothe them. They had been weighted by the thick air of the woods for the past few days, but now she felt liberated.

Kaos looked to their right and squinted into the distance. "I can just make out the town there, among those cliffs—see the smoke rising? But we aren't as close to town as I had hoped to be. Come, we'll take cover in the woods again till we're closer. It won't do to be out in the open."

He put his arm around her and started leading her back toward the woods. Evren glanced over her shoulder, feeling an ache inside her and wishing they could stay close to the water's majesty. She reminded herself that they would be setting sail soon enough, soaring freely across the waves and likely getting tired of seeing them a few days into their voyage.

They had just entered the trees' shadows when a voice called to them:

"Out in the open for once, eh, Kaos?"

Kaos' hold on Evren tensed so hard that she thought her bones would break. Then he released her and whispered sharply in her ear, "Run—"

A brilliant streak of crimson and gold shot past. Evren jumped and then stared, her heart drumming against her chest as the flames set the tree before them ablaze.

"*Run,*" Kaos repeated, more harshly than before. It was no suggestion, but a clear order.

Yet as he pushed her toward the trees and turned to face his rival, she could not run. Fear crippled her, for she knew where the fire came from. The idea of any harm consuming Kaos suddenly paralyzed her with a new, greater fear than any she had ever felt for herself. She turned and watched as Kaos marched forward.

A man stood some yards away on the sand, with the ocean at his back. His skin, hair, and eyes were an earthy brown, not as dark as Kaos', but his facial features reflected the fact that he was also a Carmennan. His tall, lithe frame differed from Kaos' stockier, broad-shouldered one, but fire danced along the edges of the long sword he held, while sparks hissed from its sharp tip.

"Running and hiding yet again?" Codyn said. "Ever your best strategy—to run from danger, from the slightest signs of confrontation, instead of meeting them head-on. But I'm certain your newest lover here has surmised that much for herself by now. Tell me, milady, what has Kaos told you of my Amata?"

He nodded in Evren's direction. Kaos whirled, looking furious that she had disobeyed his orders to run. Evren stood frozen in the shadows. Then, feeling a warmth over her heart, she remembered her sunstone. Clutching it, she marched forward to stand with Kaos.

"Don't answer him," Kaos said sharply.

Evren studied the fierceness in Kaos' gaze. Fear flickered visibly beyond his rage. Fear would destroy him—destroy both men. Codyn looked on the verge of wielding his blade and casting fire spells, but perhaps—if they could only understand one another—she could make them stop fighting before they began.

"He told me that she was his lover," Evren said, "but that you were in love with her as well. That you accidentally killed her with your dragon, and in revenge, he slayed the dragon. And that he has been running from you since, because you desire vengeance. He says the only way to stop you would be to kill you—and he doesn't want that. He loves you still—"

"*Does* he?" Codyn laughed out loud, a derisive, almost mad laugh. "The man who stole my lover, got her killed in a duel when I tried to defend her honor—then, after all that, after stealing all I had and murdering my dragon too, the one hope I had to love something again? Either Kaos has a twisted view of love, or you do, milady, or perhaps both of you do. Perhaps the two of you deserve one another after all. Perhaps I've no need to save you from his madness."

"Save me?" Evren said, glancing between Kaos and Codyn with question. "From Kaos? It's him who saved me in the first place. I don't understand. Kaos didn't get Amata killed. It was *you*—you who followed them, out of jealousy. That's what he told me."

"Of course, that's what he told you," Codyn spat, and Evren thought the flames danced a little higher across his blade. The fire in his eyes intensified, as did his disgust as he glared at Kaos. "Amata was my lover long before Kaos knew her. He didn't know this. It was she who betrayed me first, by making love to him. But even once he knew, did he tell me? No. No, he betrayed me as a brother and as a friend, continuing to see her in secret. I didn't suspect a thing until Amata announced she was running away with him...

"I followed them, yes. I followed them to win her back. I fought in her favor, in her honor. But that wasn't my idea either. I just wanted to see her. I wanted to talk to her. I wanted to try to persuade her back into my arms. It was Kaos who wanted a fight.

"Kaos hasn't been running just to spare me or whatever other noble fairy tales he has filled your pretty little head with. He has been running from the truth. The disgusting truth that he stole *my* lover from me, *my* intended, and then caused her death by fighting me for her."

Evren glanced at Kaos, ready for him to defend himself. But he said nothing, only stared at Codyn absently, as if seeing far past his words into the distant memories that created them.

"You stayed hidden for quite a while this time," Codyn continued. "You were most clever in your methods. But I knew you would be pulled toward the south. I finally caught up with you in Rozul, on the day of the slave market. You sold the dragon scale, thinking no one would know how to use its magic—but see now, that was your first mistake..." He waved his sword, grinning proudly as its flames lit the darkening sky; the palest stars shone along the fringes of the heavens. Evren clutched her sunstone even tighter, remembering the power of her own hidden flame. "Your second mistake piqued my interest but led to my own mistakes. You bought the girl here, and I decided to follow you for a time, to see what you would do. I lost track of you for a while, but then I found you again in Willardton, your old haunt..."

His gaze strayed then to Evren. His disgust deepened just a bit, but a strange admiration glinted in his eyes too. "You *do* share her likeness... But the very idea that he thinks he could mirror Amata's beauty in another sickens me. 'True' love—finding another girl to replace the one you murdered, one that looks so similar, acts similar. Yes, *that* is 'true' love indeed..."

"It's not that way," Kaos pleaded at Evren. "It started that way, yes. But I promise you, my feelings for you are genuine—"

"I don't care about that," Evren said, trying to stave the swell of emotions as the truth of Codyn's words sank in. Kaos didn't deny Codyn's story; he had lied to her. This wounded trust stung most deeply, but she pushed her hurt aside as best she could. "I don't care what you've done in your past— either of you. I just want you to stop this fighting. This hatred. This venom between you—put it to rest."

111

"See how she defends your honor, even when you've none left to defend?" Codyn sneered. "Oh, I would gladly lay this matter to rest, save that would dishonor my sweet Amata's sacrifice, and that of my dragon. Besides, it's Kaos who taught me long ago that peace and satisfaction are found only on the other side of war. He taught me that the moment he decided to fight me for Amata instead of talking like the good friends we once were."

"You're right," Kaos said weakly. "All you say is true. But it gives you no right to sabotage a town filled with innocent people —"

"*Amata* was innocent!" Codyn cried. "She was more innocent than the woman standing beside you, and you destroyed her—not for love, but for your own desires!"

"I *did* love her!" Kaos yelled back. "Don't tell me—"

Fireballs blazed through the air as Codyn swung his sword with an enraged roar. Kaos shoved Evren to the ground and raised his sword, holding it so that the flames deflected off its broad side. For a moment, Evren wondered how this was possible. Perhaps the blade's jasper stone held some power that defied dragon fire. If so, perhaps Kaos had a fighting chance after all.

Then Codyn's next attack slammed so hard into Kaos' sword that he was sent spiraling through the air, crashing into the sand and skidding on his back. Kaos pushed himself up with a groan and then leapt back to his feet, charging across the beach toward his rival.

Codyn swung his sword, releasing volley after volley of flame. Kaos dodged, ducking left and right, sometimes throwing himself to the ground, only to roll to the side as another fireball grazed the sand. Then he would leap back up to charge at Codyn again.

Codyn's attacks grew more frequent and more erratic. Frustration flooded his angry gaze as Kaos continued to weave artfully between his attacks, taking no damage and drawing ever nearer to him. Then Kaos was upon him and their swords met, screeching with the hideous song of metal against metal. Flames still blazed furiously along the edges of

Codyn's sword, but Kaos kept him so close and engaged in swordplay that his casting fire was impossible.

Codyn skipped around lithely, barely dodging many of Kaos' blows. Kaos swung his sword mercilessly, all the while ducking to the side as the flames of Codyn's blade flashed out toward him. Once or twice, Evren saw him grimace as their fire scathed his flesh, but he didn't stop or slow—

Kaos knocked Codyn's sword from his hands. The flaming blade flew like a shooting star, landing some yards away. Kaos sliced at Codyn's side, and Codyn clutched at the fresh wound with a cry of pain. Kaos' next blow landed on Codyn's leg, sending him sprawling on his back. Codyn scrambled backwards in the sand, trying to creep toward his sword but collapsing again, scrunching his face in pain. Blood smeared the golden sand, shimmering in the light of the rising moon and stars; the sun had nearly extinguished. Kaos stood over his rival, pointing his sword straight at his heart.

"I don't want to do this, Codyn," Kaos said, "but I can't let you hurt her."

"It's not her I wish to harm," Codyn gasped as he struggled for air, "anymore than I ever wished to hurt Amata or those townspeople."

"How can I know this? You attacked us in our sleep. We could have *both* died. It's over, Codyn. You won't be harming any more innocent souls. I love you, but I must do this. For her sake, and for yours...my brother..."

Kaos hesitated. He gazed down at Codyn with the same heavy remorse reflected in his voice. Then, he raised his sword—

With a cry, Codyn stretched forth his hand. Black scales sprang from the back of his hand and wrist, bristling from his skin. He yelled loudly and his face twisted with pain, but he held the spell steady until his sword zipped toward him from across the sand. He gripped it, swung it, and sent Kaos flying back with a jet of flame.

Evren had stood frozen still since the battle had begun, stunned into silence first by shock and then by fear as she prayed for Kaos' life to be spared. She had hoped the battle had come to an end with Kaos' apparent triumph. Now, as it threatened to begin anew, whatever fears had held her spellbound released their grasp on her, replaced by a more desperate fear, and she cried out,

"Kaos—Codyn—both of you, stop—please! You don't have to do this! Remember that you were once friends—!"

Her pleas went abandoned as Kaos and Codyn both leapt to their feet and their duel progressed once more.

Evren clutched her sunstone, wanting desperately to make a wish but knowing that she must save it, for even protective magics had their weaknesses. Her gem was fueled by star fire, Codyn's sword by dragon fire. Fire against fire was no fair duel; she could not be certain hers would win. She must hang on till the absolute last moment.

But it tortured her to stand helpless as Kaos dodged blow after blow of both sword and flame, or as he began to weaken and the fire grazed his arms and legs more frequently, making him grimace in pain. He staggered but then pushed through, continuing the fight.

Though Codyn reeled from his own wounds, dragging his injured leg after him, he spared no mercy in his attacks, throwing continuous volleys of flame at Kaos. This time, he let his fire magic be his shield. Kaos wove between the fiery attacks, trying to draw close enough to Codyn to resume their battle by sword, but Codyn made certain there was no room for him to do so.

Kaos burst forward, holding the broadside of his sword before him to create a makeshift shield as he charged at his rival. A large part of the fire deflected off the sword, though some of the flames grazed his arms and legs, setting bits of his tunic ablaze. The stench of burning flesh poisoned the air. Kaos pushed through, running harder. He was mere feet away from Codyn when he lifted his sword, poised to swing, and continued to charge forth.

Just as Kaos reached him, Codyn swung his sword in a wide arc, sending daggers of flame shooting in all directions. Evren ducked down and covered her face. When the shrill sound of fire zipping through the sky had vanished, she glanced up—and gasped, staring in horror.

Evren saw as the fiery darts assailed Kaos' body, making him collapse to his knees before Codyn. She watched as Kaos drove his sword through Codyn's side—just as Codyn drove his sword through Kaos' side. It happened before her in torturous slow motion, yet so fast that even her scream came a moment too late. As Kaos fell, his broad, strong figure trembled head to toe, at once consumed by a frightening weakness. Blood poured freely from his wound, between his fingers as he clutched his side, running down his tunic and staining the ground below. As Evren watched, it was like the tourniquet that had been holding all of her emotions captive was abruptly removed. As his blood ran freely, her emotions poured out in one giant, overwhelming rush as she admitted to herself, at last, how much she really loved him.

Evren fell beside him. She glanced at Codyn who had also fallen; he lay groaning, twitching grotesquely, stained with his blood and Kaos'. He reached for his sword, but Evren took it and flung it far across the sand. She did the same with Kaos' sword. Then, she looked down at Kaos.

As Kaos lay in a sea of his blood, struggling to draw each rasping breath, Evren's heart seemed to drop inside her, like the falling stars of her world. If he died, her heart would keep on falling for all eternity, ever sinking deeper and deeper into despair yet never finding the solace of reaching the bottom. She could not let this happen. She could not let him die. For her own sake and for the sake of all the good she knew he could yet do in the world. Gently, she took his face and rested his head in her lap. Then, twisting her hair to one side, she bent down, held it away from the blood, and kissed him.

Kaos pulled away with a gasp, "Evren—what are you doing?"

"Kissing you," she said. Then, with a soft smirk, "You had no problem with it several nights ago—"

"But your sunstone—*what are you doing?*"

He reached up a trembling hand and held the gem up to show her. More than its usual glisten, it had begun to glow from within, as if a tiny sun resided inside of it.

"I am imparting to you my special gift," Evren said.

"Your gift?" Kaos said, dropping his hand and wincing as his breathing grew quicker, more uneven.

"Yes... It's how I came to this world in the first place. And it is how I shall ascend now, return to live alongside my kind. I can never find Novalight again, but hopefully the Stars of *this* world will be just as accepting..."

"Slow down," Kaos said, shaking his head. He swooned at the sudden movement, and Evren held him as tightly as she could, trying to steady him. "Novalight...the stories you told—your grandmother's stories—"

"All true. Now, let me kiss you again before it's too late."

He parted his lips, perhaps to protest, perhaps to accept the gift. She kissed him before he had the chance to do either. As they kissed, she silently chanted the spell and breathed its light inside him, letting her tears fall freely as she felt the warmth of the pendant leave the place over her heart and nestle instead at his. She took his face in her hands, feeling the power of her Starfire's healing flame course through his veins and down to the core of his heart, healing every wound. Then, as soon as she was certain the spell was complete, she severed the kiss, smiled at him—

A brilliant light burst from the sunstone, traveling through the gold chain around her neck and fusing with her skin. Its bright, golden-pink rays absorbed inside her and down into the depths of her heart, making it burn with a powerful warmth. For a moment, the heat intensified to the point of pain, but then the warmth dispersed, racing through her veins and shimmering from her skin. As tiny beams of light danced along her every surface, she gazed down at her hand, turning it over and smiling at the light dancing across her skin. How good it felt to be herself once again, at long last.

"Evren…what's happening to you?"

She gazed down then at Kaos. His gaze pleaded her, but no further words were needed. He understood what was happening, even as he questioned it. A bittersweetness shot through her heart. Once more becoming what she was always meant to be liberated her, and she wished she could share this experience with him intimately. Instead, all she could do was savor this final moment and share it with him inasmuch as she was able. She hoped he would understand. She didn't have much time to try and make him.

"My wishes can only be linked to protection and healing," she said. "I saved this wish for you, knowing you would need it above all others. I wish you could know how much I love you. What you see on the surface, you would have to multiply by ten to know how much I love you, how much I kept locked away, because of fear…which seems so silly now. And then, you could multiply that number by a hundred, and that's how much I could have loved you, had you given me the chance, and how much I will love you as I watch over you now from the heavens. I do this thing now because I love you. And it because doesn't matter that you don't love me in return. Because my love for you is true, and strong enough for the both of us."

"But I do love you," he said; pain filled his gaze more deeply, and he played with a lock of her hair. "I want you to know this, Evren. If I didn't love you, I wouldn't have been so determined to keep you safe. Maybe you love me more. Maybe I was a fool not to see your love for me sooner, and maybe I don't deserve your love at all. But I *do* love you."

"I know," she said, stroking his face. "But do not say to me that you don't deserve to be loved. Love is a beautiful gift meant for everyone to share and receive. It is an unconditional gift that houses so many other wonderful gifts—compassion, forgiveness, understanding... You would not have to love me at all for me to love you. But I am glad that you do. Knowing this is the greatest gift you could have sent with me on my way to the Stars...

"I must go now. The Stars call to me, and I cannot hold on much longer. Goodbye, Kaos. I love you. Be filled with chaos no longer. Be at peace. Find the south, and choose a new name—a *good* name—and think of me as you do—"

9

In the blink of an eye, she was gone.

Kaos sat up, glancing all around him in a daze. He scrambled to his feet, whirling about, looking for her. He would have called her name, but shock seemed to have seized his ability even to speak.

As abruptly as he had noticed the absence of her, he now noticed the absence of all pain. He felt his side, where the great gash from the dragon-claw sword should yet be torn open wide, releasing his blood and poisoning it at once. He ran his hands along his arms, where fresh burns should glare up at him alongside the old scars with their haunting reminder. None of it was there anymore. All of it had vanished, along with her.

The only reason he knew that the past several months of his life had been more than a dream was the sudden feeling of something cool resting at his chest. He reached up and touched the sunstone pendant. He unclasped its chain from around his neck and held it tenderly in his palm. Its glow had vanished with its warmth, its sparkle diminished to a dull, murky lackluster.

For the first time in long months, Kaos wept freely. Because for the first time in long months, he had allowed himself to love but had only allowed himself to fully realize it now, in her death, in the sacrifice that she had made to keep him alive.

Kaos secured the pendant around his neck once more. Living seemed a pointless thing, then as now—perhaps more so, for none now remained for him to avenge, except for himself, for allowing her to make such a sacrifice in his stead. But live on he would. She had given him this gift of life, and he would not disrespect her memory by squandering it. He would seek some other noble purpose and, by the sword, live—or die—seeking to fulfill it.

Where even to begin to find such a purpose?

South. He had always been traveling south, to escape his homeland, his past—every dark thing connected to him. He had traveled south to lead Codyn away from his family, knowing Codyn would follow wherever he went and wishing that, when the time for their confrontation came, he could keep Evren safe at all costs. Now Codyn was no more, his threat destroyed forever.

North. Kaos would instead turn north. He would return to his family and spend his days making amends to them for the torment caused them, both at Codyn's hands and by his own selfish foolery.

As Kaos turned north, something seemed to call to him from the heavens—a pale pink glow. His first thought was that more time had passed in fighting Codyn than he had realized, and dawn now stole upon him. But the glow didn't shine from the horizon. Instead, it radiated from up high. He turned his gaze in its direction—

And there allowed it to linger. Linger on the perfect star bedazzling the heavens with its pink core and yellow, orange, and purple facets. More like a diamond than a star, it gleamed and twinkled, sparkled and shone— just like the sunstone she had once worn.

Kaos touched the empty gem over his heart. Suddenly, its cold seemed to diminish as he realized her warmth hovered right over him, living on inside the glorious new Star above.

"Kahlil?"

Surprise rippled inside Kaos at the familiarity of the name, as well as that of the voice who had spoken it, though the meanings of neither were immediately clear to him.

Kaos turned and saw the tall, strong Carmennan man standing some feet away, his face filled with just as great a wonder as that quickly overtaking Kaos. Then Kaos remembered and knew the man's face.

"Codyn," Kaos said. "But you…I thought you died…"

"I thought you did too," Codyn said. "It was the last thing I saw before everything turned black… I watched you fall; your blood was everywhere, and mine…But that seems suddenly a lifetime ago to me."

"And…and to me as well," Kaos said, slowly as he realized the strange sensation Codyn had already discovered for himself.

Kaos studied Codyn closely. He knew everything that had happened between them; he knew the overwhelming pain and anger that should grip him in his enemy's presence. Except the pain he still felt was not the doing of the man before him, and that man was no longer an enemy, but rather a dear old friend. This discovery was both ancient and brand new to Kaos and, in the same breath, wildly exhilarating. Kaos knew who Codyn was, just as he knew Evren was the great Star blazing above them. But he felt as though he suddenly viewed both through a magical sort of lens, one that made him see things more clearly, or perhaps just in a different light or color.

"How is this even possible?" Codyn breathed.

"Evren," Kaos said, and when Codyn frowned in confusion, he added, "the woman who was with me."

"Where is she now?"

Kaos nodded toward the Star blazing bright and bold overhead. "Up there. Watching over us."

Codyn followed Kaos' gaze and shook his head, looking even more overwhelmed. "I don't…I don't understand…"

"She was a Star. She was a mysterious creature, and a pure soul. A true healer with a most beautiful spirit. She used the last of her wishes to save us, I think."

Kaos and Codyn watched Evren's Star for a little while longer. Kaos basked in its shimmering beauty, allowing the memory of her love and goodness and all she had been to fill him. As with Codyn, thinking of her this way was strangely not only a memory, but a discovery as well. As if he had known all along what she was but could only now, on the other side of this bizarre rebirth, truly see her with his more perfected heart and purified spirit.

"You are no longer called 'Kahlil,'" Codyn said. "'Kaos,' they said your name was, in Willardton."

Kaos nodded. "I changed my name after Amata's death, after everything unraveled between you and me. I didn't know peace for a long time. But now Evren has given me—has given us—this new chance. A chance for new life and reconciliation. She wished me to take a new name. In a way, it was like my last promise to her. I think I shall once more take one of the names of our people." He looked over at his friend. "Kahoku, I will now be called. Kahoku Jahan Jaspar."

"Kahoku Jahan," Codyn said, meeting his gaze. "You name yourself in her honor."

Kahoku nodded. "But I keep the name of my brothers as well. I am still forever a 'Jaspar.'"

The two shared a grin.

Codyn returned his gaze to the heavens. His face pulled into a pensive frown, and he shook his head slowly. "It's so hard to fathom...The person I was, when I was lost in my own sort of chaos...I see everything so clearly now, that it feels an entire lifetime ago, as if it all happened to someone else, not to me. Except that the memories linger clear as day, and with them, some of the pain. What a true and wondrous lady your Evren must have been. To use her wish not only for *your* healing, but for *ours*..."

"A true lady she was indeed," Kahoku said, touching the empty sunstone; its coldness mirrored the loneliness still lingering inside his heart, though at the same time, the warmth of her Star above strengthened him. He had expected to feel *less* without her beside him, but this was different than when Amata had died. Evren had sacrificed herself for him, so that he could only feel *more*. To do otherwise would be to dishonor Evren and her gift—and to betray his own love for her. Her Star shone brightly, its rays seeming to dance and extend themselves toward him. He wondered if she could hear them, hear *him*—even his own thoughts—and if she tried to reach out to him, to comfort him. It was just the sort of thing she would do, that she had always done—putting his needs above her own.

"You know," Codyn said, "when I fell from your last blow, when I blacked out, I truly thought I was dead. But then a vision came to me. A vivid dream, so vivid I thought I had, by some miracle, been allowed inside the Forever Havens after all. I was clad in a bright blue and silver tunic. I wore the crest of the Lozolian Echelon across my breast. I knelt before a beautiful queen, a Mira Elf, judging by her sunlit hair. 'Lia,' she called herself. I was receiving some kind of high honors, and all her people cheered. The dream was like the visions I used to have as a child...

"And then I woke up. I woke up and realized I wasn't dead at all, that I was perfectly healed. I can't help but wonder if the vision was somehow part of Evren's magic. I felt a sense of great destiny during the vision, and even now. There was a realness to it, a calling. Whether this calling is real, or simply born from my sudden desire for redemption, I don't know. I don't understand how I could ever be hailed as a hero, after all the evil I've wielded, the pain I've dealt. And yet, I can't help but feeling like I did as a child."

"Your visions always *did* come true," Kahoku said. "It seems Evren healed more than our bodies. It seems she healed our spirits as well. And maybe, with your newfound clarity, you can now see some purpose you are meant to achieve, some great destiny you could never pursue while consumed in your anger and grief."

Codyn shook his head and heaved a great sigh. "I don't know... I *want* to hope. But how can a man—a knight, no less—wreak such destruction, fracture his spirit till it's barely recognizable...and then hope to create something good from it?"

"I don't know either," Kahoku said. "But Evren saved us for a reason, and I intend to find out what that is—even if I must spend my life fighting for it. Maybe she simply wanted to see us reconcile, or maybe there's something more. Whatever the case, I too see more clearly now. You weren't the only man in the wrong. I was self-righteous at times, a coward, and selfish. I should never have run from you. I should have confronted you, brother to brother. I brought great danger to many innocent lives—the entirety of Willardton—and to Evren. I told myself buying her from the slave market was the noble thing to do. But really, I hoped to atone for my sins against Amata. And against you. It was selfish to get her involved, knowing you still sought vengeance. I should never have taken her with me...and now she is gone..."

"And we remain," Codyn said. "I don't know what comfort we can take in that. Except it seems that Amiel still has some purpose for us...whatever that may be."

Kahoku drew his sword then and raised it toward Codyn. "We once swore an oath of eternal brotherhood. An oath to love, honor, and protect one another until the sun sets on our time in this world and the great silver stags come to guide our souls to an eternal rest. Perhaps we should remember that oath now. Perhaps we could start anew and hold one another to it more perfectly this time."

Codyn drew his sword and crossed it with Kahoku's. "Brother to brother, under the light of Amiel's wings."

"Brother to brother," Kahoku said, "under the light of Amiel's wings."

They sheathed their swords, grasped hands, and pulled each other into a tight embrace.

When they pulled back from one another, Codyn said, "I hardly know where to start. Perhaps in Willardton. The freshest wounds were made there and may yet be fixed. Perhaps I can work my way backward from there."

"I will come with you," Kahoku said. "I will stand by your side and be the friend you always deserved. I will strive to be a true knight, to know true courage. I will follow you to the farthest corners of the earth, and to its bitter end."

"And I you."

They shared a grin, a solemn expression, but one lit with a greater hope and determination than Kahoku had ever been able to feel as Kaos.

"Well then," Codyn said. "Shall we start walking?"

"We shall," Kahoku said, leading the way across the beach toward the forest. "And who knows? We can never be certain what wish Evren made. Perhaps we may return to Willardton and find it healed as well."

"Perhaps," Codyn said, "though if she is as wise as you seem to believe, doing so might make things too easy for us."

"Perhaps, or perhaps not—I think we've many years' work ahead of us, either way."

"But at least we shall face them together this time."

Kahoku nodded. "Well said, my friend."

They passed under the shadows of the tree line. Just before they crossed into the forest, Kahoku paused and turned to look up at Evren's Star. A fear had flitted through him that, as he and Codyn reconciled, it might disappear, its magic no longer needed. But as it twinkled brightly, he knew Evren would remain to watch over them for a long time to come. He knew her lifetime was many of theirs. And he could almost imagine, intermingled with the stars, a vision of himself, though not as he was now, as Kahoku. He imagined he could see Kaos, the person he had been only moments yet lifetimes ago, the man who had had to die so that Kahoku could be born. He imagined that he could see Evren too, holding Kaos' hand, and that they both smiled down at him.

Kahoku smiled back at them. He raised his hand in a sign of farewell. Then he turned and followed his friend into the woods, into the first chapter of their new adventure together.

Ballad of the Knight in Rusted Armor

Said the knight in rusted armor
After he had played his part,
"Oh, sweet damsel, do not love me,
For you see I have no heart.

"True, it may be that I saved you,
As my honor doth decree,
But my heart was stolen long ago
Never to return to me."

"But if I could only find it,"
Said the maiden pure and fair,
For an aching in her heart told her
It must be found somewhere.

"Any hope you feel is futile,
For no matter where you seek,
If you find it, it's still broken;
Do not think to set me free."

But the maiden was undaunted;
Through their questing she did see
If his heart could be restored
The kind of man that he could be.

With her sweet, strong spirit she lured him
Safely back into the light
His heart was found, sealed and made whole,
Bringing death to his dark plight.

Then said the knight in shining armor
Once the maiden had played her part,
"Oh, sweet damsel, how I love thee,
Now I give to you my heart.

"Forevermore I'll love you
And hold you in my arms;
My knight and lover's honor
Will now shield you from all harm."

One Starry Knight

The maiden gave him everything,
Surrendering her life,
And he in turn gave all he had
To claim her as his wife.

And so they lived most merrily,
Their hearts to each other won;
But call this not a happy ending,
For their fairy tale's just begun.

Dear Reader,

Thanks so much for taking the time to read my book! Creating *One Starry Knight* was a very personal journey inspired by the first man I ever truly, unconditionally loved. Evren reflects all of the love and pain, twists and turns that I went through with my real-life Kaos, and the story is like my own fairy tale brought to life. I wanted it to be more than a romance, because the real-life Kaos is a very deep and spiritual man; hence, I wanted it to have a more spiritual meaning. Also, yes, that is me posing as Evren in the photos; she's still my favorite original character to cosplay!

Kahoku has since become one of my favorite characters to write, so I'll let you in on a secret: He'll be appearing again in the last book of my series, *The Gailean Quartet,* as well as another series I currently have in the works!

If you'd like to help a girl out, please leave a review for me on Amazon! I absolutely love hearing from my readers. Discovering a new review and reading what others have to say about my books truly makes my day. It also helps other awesome readers like you to discover my book so they can enjoy it too!

On that note, God bless, happy reading, and may you be inspired! I look forward to seeing you in my next book.

~ Christine E. Schulze

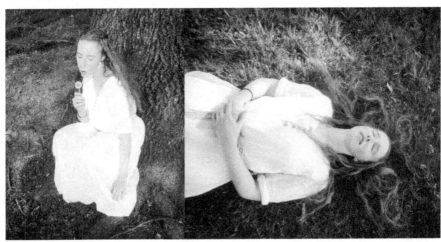

Photos courtesy of Sarah Jolly

The *One Starry Knight* *Artists*

I want to give a special thanks to all of my artists, including Sarah Jolly, one of my besties, for helping me make this book a reality. While it might not be my greatest work in the sense that it may never become my best-selling or most popular, it's one of my greatest works in the sense that it is my heart. Thanks to all the following for helping me bring this very special, personal story to life through your beautiful artwork. Thanks also to everyone for being on time! There were a lot of you, and I know my schedule was a bit last-minute for some, but everyone pulled through, and I truly appreciate it. God bless you all!

Page 5: Tiffany Tutti

Page 6: India Emmaline (Indiemme on Instagram)

Page 10: India Emmaline (Indiemme on Instagram)

Page 17: India Emmaline (Indiemme on Instagram)

Page 20: Sarah Jolly

Page 25: Sarah Jolly

Page 29: Sarah Jolly

Page 35: Karen Swartz

Page 41: Maria Lia Malandrino (mlm_illustration on Instagram)

Page 43: Aeli

Page 48: Heisedebao on Instagram (Black-pantheress on DeviantArt)

Page 51: Aeli

Page 57: Berruppy on Instagram

Page 60: Gabrijela Ester (Orlia.art on Instagram, Orlia Ester on Youtube)

About the Author

Christine E. Schulze has been living in castles, exploring magical worlds, and creating fantastical romances and adventures since she was too young to even write of such stories. Her collection of YA, MG, and children's fantasy books, *The Amielian Legacy*, is comprised of series and stand-alone books that can all be read separately but also weave together to create a single, amazing fantasy.

One of her main aspirations for *The Amielian Legacy* is to create fantasy adventures with characters that connect with readers from many different backgrounds. Her current focus is to include racially diverse characters and also those with disabilities. The latter is inspired by Schulze working with adults with autism and other developmental disabilities at Trinity Services in Southern Illinois. She also donates 25% of her royalties to ALFA, a local charity that supports many of Trinity's programs.

Schulze draws much of her inspiration from favorite authors like Tolkien and Diana Wynne Jones, favorite games like *The Legend of Zelda*, and especially from the people in her life. Some of her exciting ventures include the publication of her award-winning *Bloodmaiden*, as well as *The Stregoni Sequence* with Writers-Exchange. Her books for younger readers include *In the Land of Giants* and *The Amazing Captain K.*

Christine currently lives in Belleville, IL, but you can visit her on her website: http://christineschulze.com

The Amielian Legacy

More Books by Christine E. Schulze

The Amielian Legacy is a vast fantasy comprised of both stand-alone books and series for children and young adults. *The Amielian Legacy* creates a fantastical history for North America in much the same way that Tolkien's Middle Earth created a mythology for Europe. While it's not necessary to read any particular book or series to read the others, they do ultimately weave together to create a single overarching fantasy.

~*~*~ Children's Books ~*~*~

The Adventures of William the Brownie

The Special Needs Heroes Collection

In the Land of Giants

The Puzzle of the Two-Headed Dragon

The Amazing Captain K

Puca: A Children's Story About Death

~*~*~ Young Adult Books ~*~*~

The Amielian Legends: A Young Adult Fantasy Collection

(Can be read in any order)

The Chronicles of the Mira

The Crystal Rings

Bloodmaiden

One Starry Knight

Lily in the Snow
One Starry Knight
Tales from the Lozolian Realm
The Pirates of Meleeon

The Gailean Quartet

(First release April 2020)

Prelude of Fire
Serenade of Kings
Symphony of Crowns
Requiem of Dragons

The Stregoni Sequence

Golden Healer, Dark Enchantress
Memory Charmer
Wish Granter and Other Enchanted Tales